Dead Letters

Dead Letters

Francis King

First published in Great Britain in 1998 by
ALLISON & BUSBY Limited
114 New Cavendish Street
London W1M 7FD

Copyright © 1998 by FRANCIS KING

The right of Francis King
to be identified as author of this work has been asserted
by him in accordance with the Copyright, Designs and Patents Act 1988

A catalogue record for this book is available from the British Library

ISBN 0 74900 374 X

Design and cover illustration: PEPE MOLL

Edited by Alba Editorial, S. L.

Printed in Great Britain by
Biddles Limited, Guildford and King's Lynn

For Lenore Denny

Usually Faith writes all Steve's letters for him. He suffers from what he has by now learned to call dyslexia, and if he has to write a letter, pondering if he has spelled the shortest and easiest words correctly and constantly consulting the little pocket dictionary which he carries about with him, all too soon his still handsome face grows congested, the sweat breaks out on his forehead, and his heart begins to race.

But this letter he must, must write himself, even if later he asks Faith to check everything in it for him. By now the garage is shut and Faith has gone home ahead of him, because tonight is the night when she has a monthly hen party with some of the 'girls' (that is how they still talk of themselves) whom she knew at secretarial college. Faith is getting stout, but she retains a sturdy comeliness. Steve sometimes wishes that he could love her more, just as he often wishes that he could love other people – his children, his mother, his sister, his closest buddies – more.

He twists the top of the biro and twists it again, in an agony of how to get started. It is hard enough for him to write to a relative or a friend. To write to a stranger, like this Englishman, fills him with anxiety and dread. He bends over the sheet of lined paper, torn from a school exercise book jettisoned by his youngest son. Eventually, with much thought and with repeated flickings through the pages of the dictionary, he wrings out the following:

I write to acknowledge receipt of your letter of October 14th. I wish that I could be of assistance to you with your biography of the Prince, but the truth is that I hardly knew him. When I was a young man, I met him by chance and he invited me back to stay because it was raining and I had nowhere else to go. He and the Princess were very kind to me, but it is now so long a time ago and in any case I saw little of them, spending most of my time on sight-seeing and wandering about Palermo and so on.

The Prince and the Princess were both real aristocrats. Of course I never guessed then that, after his death, his novel would be so successful and that he would become famous all over the world. Even here, in this little backwater, they showed the film and many people went to it!

I really have nothing more to say, I'm afraid . . .

At that point Steve breaks off. He holds what he has written up to the brilliant cone of light from the Anglepoise lamp on Faith's desk and, brows knit and lips moving, reads over, with extreme difficulty, what he has written.

He sighs and rubs the back of his right hand up and down a cheek bristling at this late hour with stubble. It's not right, not right at all . . .

In anguish and exasperation he decides that he will have to try again.

1975

I

The short, plump, elderly man in the black Homburg hat and the shiny black overcoat reaching below his calves, peered out from under the ancient, horn-handled umbrella which protruded one dislocated elbow askew, and stared at a pair of hands. He shuffled on over the slithery pavement, hesitated, turned back. To the owner of the hands, cowled under an anorak hood, bare, muscular, sunburned legs stuck out from a bench in indifference to the downpour, he said something in Italian in a nasally resonant voice.

Steve gazed up with eyes of an extraordinarily pale blue and said: 'Sorry. I don't speak Italian. Only English. *Scusi.*'

He had been sitting there, his backpack beside him, waiting in resigned, weary patience for a bus. An elderly woman in a plastic overcoat and hood, many minutes – twenty, thirty, forty? – before, had told him that a number 42 would take him to the youth hostel on the other side of the town. Irene had said that she was sorry, she could not drive him there, it was too far, she must catch that ferry if she was not to be late for her appointment in Naples. Or was it Florence, or Rome, or Venice? He had hitch-hiked and bussed in such a brief space of time to so many places not merely in Italy but all over Europe that the names now glittered and scraped together, so many jumbled shards of glass, in a brain dulled by fatigue and depression. Irene had talked incessantly, against a background of music, during the three days between her picking him up by one roadside and abandoning him by another. He was not sure if he found this following silence comforting or eerie.

The old man hesitated, peering, head bent sideways. He gave the umbrella a brisk shake and drops of rain spattered off it. Then he asked: 'You're an American?'

'No. I'm from Australia.'

'From Australia! Do you know, I can't have met more than a dozen Australians in my whole life!' He spoke English with only rare mistakes and with almost no trace of an accent. Later, he was to reveal that his mother had been English. 'Patrick White,' he said. 'I'm a great admirer of Patrick White.'

Steve had nothing to say to that.

The Italian went on: 'If you're waiting for a bus, it's useless for you to sit here. Sunday. No bus.'

'But someone I asked told me . . .'

The Italian said: 'In Sicily people tell you not the truth but what they think you want to hear. As in Ireland.' He folded the umbrella and sat down on the bench beside the boy. He exuded a smell of eau-de-Cologne and another, less pleasant, sweet-sour odour which the eau-de-Cologne could not wholly mask. Tilting his plump body to one side, grunting with the effort, he drew out a large, monogrammed handkerchief from a trouser pocket, removed his gold-rimmed glasses and began carefully to wipe first one lens and then the other.

'Where do you want to go?'

'To the youth hostel.'

'A long way.' The Italian raised a hand and waggled it in the direction of where the hostel must lie.

'Unfortunately I don't have my car with me. I never liked driving and, since I had a small accident, I truly hate it. That car is always breaking down.' He sighed. 'Like its owner. We are both too old. My wife says we must buy a new car. But, as I said, I hate driving. So what is the point? I'm happier to take buses – or taxis.' He turned. 'Do you drive?'

'Yes, I can drive.'

'All the young can drive nowadays.' He peered down at the backpack, bunching his mouth, screwing up his eyes and tilting his head first to one side and then to the other, as though he had never seen one before. 'That's all your luggage, is it?'

'Yep. That's right. All my luggage.'

'When my wife and I travel – even to our country house for a week or even a weekend – you wouldn't believe how many suitcases we have with us. Hers, not mine! And the dogs – three dogs. Pekineses.' He gave a high-pitched laugh. 'You travel light,' he said. 'You're strong,' he added. 'To carry that.' He indicated the backpack with the ferrule of his umbrella.

'I'm used to it.'

'This is the weekend. And it's getting late. I'm afraid the hostel may be full.'

Steve shrugged. He had thought of that already. In summer, youth hostels were not easy to get into.

'Then what will you do?'

'I suppose I'll have to look for a cheap lodging. Or doss down somewhere. Perhaps the station. Except that I don't know where the station is.' He had dossed down in other stations, on a bench or on a concrete floor, his body, taut even in sleep, propped against the backpack.

The old man drew a deep sigh. Then he said: 'I could offer you a bed for the night.'

'Oh, no . . . That's very kind of you. But I couldn't . . .'

'It's not much of a room. Above the garage. Our chauffeur – when we had a chauffeur – used to sleep there. But at least it's dry. And it has what are nowadays called its own "facilities". Why not accept my offer?' He was getting to his feet, opening the ancient, voluminous umbrella with the dark green sheen to its black. 'No strings attached.'

Silent, reluctant, Steve rose, stooped for the backpack, shouldered it.

Under the dripping trees of the avenue up which they walked, the light was of that same dark green shade as the sheen of the umbrella. From the open window of a tall, narrow house, notes of music from an untuned piano cascaded down in a blur of dissonance. The Italian, who had furled his umbrella when an upward glance, round head tilted on fleshily creased neck, had assured him that the rain had ceased to fall, pulled a face: 'Liszt. B minor sonata. Opus 168. But what a barbarous way to play it! Dreadful, dreadful.'

Steve sighed. The three days of driving south with Irene had been accompanied by opera on one tape after another. 'I'm a tremendous opera buff,' she had said more than once. The opera, too, had been dreadful. Through all the bellowing and screeching she had talked on and on – about her boss in the rag trade, an American, who was an absolute shit; about her divorced father and mother, he remarried to a bitch, a real bitch, in Paris, she alone in sheltered housing in Salisbury; about the flat from which she kept telling herself that she really must make a move; about the man with whom she had once shared it until she had realised that he, too, like her boss, was a shit, an absolute shit . . .

'You haven't told me your name.'

'Steve. Steve Alban.'

'How strange! *Una coincidenza.* My name is Stefano.' Then, realising that the boy could not see any coincidence between Steve and Stefano, he added: 'In Italian Steve – Stephen – is Stefano. We have the same name.'

There was a silence.

'What should I call you?'

'I've told you! Stefano.'

'Yes, but I mean . . .'

'My family name is – Torre della Aquila.' As though embarrassed, the old man came out with the grandiloquent title. 'But you don't have to worry about that. Just call me Stefano.'

Steve was never to learn to call him just that.

'Alban! Alban? How do you spell that?' Then, when Steve had told him, he asked: 'Is that a common name in Australia?'

'No, not at all common. We must be the only family with that name. Lithuanian. It's Lithuanian. And it's not even common in Lithuania.'

'Lithuanian! Then you're not really an Australian?' The tone suggested that he had caught Steve out in some imposture.

'I think that I am!' Steve raised a shoulder, to ease the pain of the strap of the backpack biting into it. 'I was born there. English is the language I speak – I know hardly any Lithuanian. I have an Australian passport.'

'So your family were refugees?'

'Yes, my father managed to escape from Lithuania.'

'From the Communists.'

'Yes. I suppose so. From the Communists.' He had always avoided discussing with his father a past of slipping across borders, languishing in refugee camps, stowing away on a Dutch freighter, and eventually finding work as a labourer, even though he had once been a student of the violin, on a building-site in Melbourne. Why? When people put that question to him, Steve would always answer: 'I don't know. I just don't know,' and frown briefly and then give a nervous laugh. He could not speak of the mingling of awe, depression, resentment and panic with which any thought of his father and his father's briefly heroic past now filled him.

'And your mother is also from Lithuania?'

'That's right. But she came to Australia earlier than my father – as a teenager, just after the War.'

Suddenly he became conscious that, as they walked along at a pace irritatingly slower than that to which he was used, the Italian had turned his head and, under the black Homburg hat with the wide brim, was peering at him. Then he said: 'I have never seen eyes like yours. Such a blue! An arctic blue.'

'My mother has the same eyes.'

'You have a typically Slav face.'

'Have I?'

'Those cheekbones. Slav cheekbones. You look as I've always imagined Prince Myshkin to have looked. Except that you look so healthy. A picture of health. One cannot imagine you having an epileptic fit.'

Steve had no idea who Prince Myshkin was. He said

nothing.

'We're almost there. You must be tired. Carrying that – that thing.'

'Oh, I'm used to it. In Australia I belong to a tramping association.'

'A tramping association?'

'That's what I enjoy most of all. I'm not really interested in buildings – all these old buildings in Europe. I like forests – and mountains – and lakes . . .' Suddenly, he was thinking of Switzerland and the piercing and yet consoling air of the Bernese Oberland, of an impulsive dip, in nothing but his Y-fronts, in an icy stream, of the sudden smell of pine as he descended down a precipitous path into the small bowl of a valley echoing with the scrape and clatter of his boots.

'That is where I used to live.' Stefano pointed across to the other side of the avenue. 'Bombed by the Americans in the last War. We never had enough money to repair it. So we left it as it is. Perhaps one day . . . But I don't think so. Other people in Palermo get richer and richer but we get poorer and poorer.'

'You once lived *there?*' Steve halted and stared across at the roofless, smoke-blackened ruin, its window-frames darned with threads of barbed wire and its vast *porte-cochère* lurching at an angle, as though at any moment about to slither away and smash into fragments. 'It looks like – like a palace.'

Stefano smiled to himself. 'Well,' he said. 'Yes. Ah, well.'

They continued on up the dripping avenue, the Italian's breath becoming more and more noisily asthmatic. He raised a hand and emitted a rasping cough behind it. Then he said: 'Our present dwelling is rather less, er, pretentious, as you can see.'

This ochre-coloured, late nineteenth-century building, here and there blotched with brown patches where its tall, grim façade had absorbed the rain, also struck Steve as looking like a palace. They climbed the wide, slippery marble steps, Stefano pausing twice, hand to serpentine brass rail, to gasp for breath. The door, with its surround of heavily carved oak-leaves and acorns, had a huge keyhole, the olive green paint chipped around it. Stefano handed his umbrella to Steve. 'Please. Please take this.' Then he fumbled, plump body twisted sideways, in one pocket of that greatcoat which enveloped him to well below his calves, and pulled out a vast, rusty key. He inserted it, turned it. '*Ecco!*'

They stepped into a hall which, Steve thought, might have been a grotto, so cavernously did it arch over their heads and so damp was its air. Beyond and to the right of the wide sweep of the staircase, he could see a courtyard, with a fountain in its centre, where a triton, nose and half his upper lip chipped away, upturned an empty horn into a shell-shaped basin teeming with weeds. On the left there was a door with a brass plaque on it – *Assicurazione Garibaldi*. There had been a similar plaque at the top of the steps.

A woman's voice, deep and plangent, called from above: 'Stefano!' The accent was Scandinavian, though Steve was not to know that. She added something in Italian, the voice going up on a note of interrogation. Soon after that a dog began to yap in increasing frenzy.

Stefano shouted back in Italian, and she shouted down again. Another dog had joined in the yapping.

'My wife still has one of her patients with her.'

Steve longed to ease off his backpack. 'Is she a doctor?'

'No. I wish she were! Then I shouldn't have to spend so much money on doctors for my wretched lungs. She's a psychoanalyst, the only Freudian psychoanalyst in Sicily. And a psychoanalyst wouldn't be able to do anything for me at my age, even if she were to decide to attempt to do so. Which is highly unlikely,' he added, giving a sudden smile. He removed his hat and then his overcoat, throwing each in turn on to a chest, across the top of which circulars and newspapers were already scattered at random. 'Let me show you your quarters. Later, after we have eaten, Guido can make up a bed for you and – and put out some towels for you – and so forth and so forth.'

On the right of the courtyard there was a terrace, with overgrown bushes, many of them shrivelled for lack of watering, in huge ceramic pots ranged symmetrically down each side. There was also a table, made of a slab of marble, a deep fissure zigzagging across it, placed on a wrought-iron frame, and some deckchairs. What Steve could not see, since the terrace was so high, was the highway and, beyond it, the sluggish, yellowish-brown sea. On the left of the courtyard was an oblong concrete box, with two wooden doors set side by side, one higher and narrower than the other. The higher, narrower door led to a garage which gave, through double-doors, on to a side street. The other door led to a sheer, cramped staircase.

'Go ahead of me, ahead of me. I must take my time. Please!'

Steve went ahead, his backpack scraping the wall now on one side of him and now on the other with each step. Behind him he could hear his host's effortful breathing.

'It's not much of a room.'

Stefano was right. But Steve had occupied far worse both in Australia and on his travels.

'It's fine,' Steve said, easing off the backpack. 'And at least I won't be woken by other people returning late and drunk or snoring all through the night.' Stefano frowned in puzzlement. 'At the youth hostels,' Steve explained. 'It'll be terrific to be alone. I like being alone.'

'And I hate it.' The old man stared at the bed, its mattress rolled up and a long, hard bolster and a pillow at its end. 'Yet nowadays' – he sighed and his eyelids and the corners of his mouth went down in wincing self-pity – 'it's a condition which increasingly afflicts me. One's friends wither and die. And to make new friends . . . Not easy.' Now he bent his body to peer under the bed. 'These days Guido is useless. Seventy-seven. I'd pension him off but he doesn't want that, poor fellow. Wife dead, son and grandchildren in America.'

'If you show me where to find a hoover – or a broom – I can do some cleaning myself.'

Stefano laughed. 'You'll have to ask Guido! Or my wife. I've no idea. I'm a spoiled old man, I'm afraid.' He went out of the door and then called over his shoulder: 'Let me see if there are any towels in the bathroom.' Steve followed him out on to the landing, and watched as the old man opened the door opposite to the bedroom. 'Well, there's *something* here. But whether it's clean or not . . .'

'It doesn't matter. I've a towel with me.'

'At least there's some *carta toeletta* – lavatory paper.'

'I have some of that with me too.'

'You have everything in that thing of yours!' He shut

the door of the bathroom and then turned and gave Steve a slow and singularly sweet smile, his sad, vaguely dissatisfied, vaguely embittered face quickly acquiring a radiance and then no less quickly losing it, as though a lamp had been clicked on and then at once clicked off in a heavily curtained room. 'Guido can bring the sheets later and make up the bed.'

'Oh, I can do that! Or use my sleeping-bag. There's no need . . .'

'Well, you can help Guido make up the bed, if you wish.' Again that singularly sweet smile briefly irradiated the brooding, sallow face. 'Now what about food?' He looked at his watch. 'Ten to eight. My wife should have finished with this patient at seven thirty. She's far too conscientious.' He delivered that verdict not in praise but in complaint. 'Fancy seeing someone on Sunday just because he says that's the only day he can spare the time. What's he doing on his other evenings? Visiting his mistress?' He laughed at the absurdity of it. 'Anyway . . . We can't eat until my wife has finished with her patient because she is the one who cooks since Guido's wife died. If you can call it cooking,' he added. 'We'll have to wait for her. On her?' he asked, for once unsure of his English. Steve made no reply, heaving the backpack on to the bed. 'Anyway . . . Why don't you begin to unpack that thing, while I get on with some work – or try to get on with some work? Then come and join me in my study for a drink. Do you think that you can find your way back to the entrance hall?'

'Of course!' How could he mistake it, when the only alternatives were either that other, high, narrow door which he had been told led to the garage, or across the gravel and up on to the terrace?

'Well, when you get there, go up the staircase to the mezzanine.'

'Mezzanine?'

For a second Stefano looked exasperated. 'Between the ground floor and the first floor. On the left, you'll see a door. My study. Join me there. Right? On the left.' The tone had become peremptory.

'Right.'

Alone, Steve crossed over to the window and watched the grey rain slowly falling out of a grey sky on to the marble of the terrace and the gravel of the courtyard. The choked basin of the fountain was now overflowing, the water splashing out of it. Beyond the terrace he could see a violet-grey plume of smoke, rising and disintegrating. Since he did not know that the sea lay over there, he did not know that the plume of smoke came from a passing tanker.

He was remembering how he had stood by the roadside, choked by the fumes of the passing cars and the dust raised off the dun fields by the high wind – the sirocco, Irene called it – which made his face tingle and his bare arms and legs unaccountably itch. His backpack was beside him. Bastards! There were cars with only a single driver at the wheel. There were vast, lumbering trucks with ample space for another passenger in the cabin or perched up on top of their cargo of vegetables, spare parts or bottles in the rear. There was a box-like little car with an English number-plate, an elderly man and woman in front and no one behind, which slowed almost to a halt beside him and then, after a hurried scrutiny by the couple, jerked off with a screech of tyres, the gritty dust billowing up behind.

After more than an hour – by now he was perched on a rock by the roadside, jumping up only when he glimpsed a likely car approaching – he saw a red dot at the point where, in the far distance, the two sides of the long, straight road eventually produced the illusion of converging, and he knew, knew at once, as he often knew on these occasions, that this time he was going to be lucky. Once again he jumped off the rock and stationed himself just before the lay-by. He extended a thumb, as the car, a large, low-slung one, with a blunt nose – yes, a Citroën, he recognised – raced towards him. The panama hat, jauntily tipped over the forehead, and the open-necked, check shirt made him at first think that the driver was a man. The car slowed, with a screeching of brakes, halted. The driver leaned across and opened the door. Then a woman's voice, raspingly impatient, called: 'Jump in! *Entrez!*' Seeing the backpack, she exclaimed: 'Oh, Christ! That'll never fit in the boot.'

'I think it'll fit in the back. Just about.' His tired, dusty, handsome face smiled in apology. 'Sorry. Thanks.'

Seeing that face and seeing the muscular brown arms struggling to get the cumbersome backpack through the door and on to the seat behind her, she said gaily: 'Not to worry! Push that carrier bag to one side. I bought myself a picnic lunch at a supermarket in Rouen. Seemed better than wasting a lot of time and money in a restaurant. I have more than I can eat. We can share it later.' He had now clambered into the seat next to her. He knew that, having been stuck so long by the roadside, he must be smelling of sweat. He hoped that the sweat would not upset her. A few days before, the Cockney driver of an articulated lorry, in a soggy, khaki-coloured singlet which revealed matted chest-hair and heavily tattooed arms, had remarked, as Steve had climbed into his cab: 'You've got a good old pong on you, haven't you, mate?' and had then roared with laughter. The driver too had had a good old pong on him.

'Where are you going?'

'South.'

'South? Can't you be a little more precise?'

'Just south. Nowhere in particular. Well, I'd like to get to Sicily in the end. Then maybe I'll move on to Greece. Turkey. Egypt.'

The woman, who must have been in her late forties and who had strong, regular features, and small, hooded eyes, stared ahead of her in silence for some time. She drove expertly. She also drove extremely fast, far beyond the speed limit. Then she said: 'I have business in Milan, Florence, Rome, Naples and Palermo. Do those places interest you?'

He was taken aback. He had not thought of her as a permanent companion on his travels. Part of him, fatigued with too much change and effort, welcomed the idea of being carried on and on to all of those places listed in the itinerary which he had sketched in at the back of a guidebook instructing travellers like him on how to survive on twenty dollars per day. Part of him – the part which caused people to describe him, sometimes in admiration and sometimes in exasperation, as a loner – shrank from the loss of his much-prized independence.

'Do they?'

He nodded. 'Yep. Yep. Those are all places that I was

planning to visit. Yep.'

'Yep.' She repeated the word derisively. Then she gave a clear laugh. Later, he was to decide that that laugh, so natural, so good-natured, so warm, was probably the most attractive thing about her. It was certainly more attractive than the deep, over-loud voice, which acquired a rasping edge when she wanted something more quickly than she was likely to get it. 'Well, that's fine then,' she said. 'You have a lift all the way. I have a companion.' She turned her head to smile at him, even as she was overtaking a lorry. 'Isn't it?'

'Yes. That's terrific.'

'Say it as though you meant it!'

Having left the car, grey with dust, on the hard shoulder of the Corniche, they settled themselves on a blanket – amazingly soft to the touch, Steve thought – down in a hollow, under some trees. 'We must have the blanket,' she had said. 'The ants here are fiendish. I know from past experience.'

She was amazed when, shaking his head, he said: 'Thank you, no, I don't drink,' as she held out a glass of wine to him. 'Well, you *are* a good boy!' she exclaimed sarcastically.

'Well, sometimes I have a pint,' he conceded.

'Unfortunately I don't have a pint with me.'

He noticed, looking down, the ugliness of the bare legs – shapeless, shiny, blue-veined – stretched out before him. But the feet, small, each nail carefully lacquered to look as though it were a shaving of mother-of-pearl, were, yes, beautiful. He noticed other people's feet, just as they in turn seemed to notice his hands. More than once a woman had told him that his hands, with their long fingers, oval nails and impression of unassailable competence and strength, were beautiful. His last girl-friend, Sue, on the initial occasion when they had gone to bed together, had amazed him by kneeling beside him, taking his hands in hers, and placing her lips first to one and then to the other in an act of illusory submission. It was something she was repeatedly to do again in the future. Indeed, he often thought that his hands were what Sue cherished most about him. Suddenly, when they were doing something as mundane as watching television together, having breakfast or travelling in a bus, she would take up one or other, draw it slowly towards her, at the same time gazing intently at him, and then rest it against her mouth, her cheek, her breast. Sometimes she would even close her eyes, as though giddy with happiness, at the moment of contact.

It was soon after lunch that the engine whirred, clattered ominously and then phutted into silence. 'Oh God!' Irene exclaimed. 'What now? We'll have to find the Italian equivalent of the AA. Did you see any telephones by the roadside? There must have been some but I can't remember any.'

'Perhaps I can fix it.'

'*You?*'

He turned his head, as he was getting out of the car, and smiled. 'No promises.'

'I hope you won't make things worse. Do you know anything, anything at all about cars?'

'Something.' He grinned.

She watched him as he tugged at his T-shirt, struggled out of it and chucked it, overarm, into the back of the car. He was aware of her watching him. It made him feel vaguely uneasy. She continued to watch him, each time that he came into view, now from around the raised bonnet in front and now from the open boot behind. Stationary under the brilliant afternoon glare, the car became extremely hot, even with all its doors open. She jerked a handkerchief out of her bag and patted at forehead, cheeks, chin, and then felt with distaste the dampness of the handkerchief on her palm. Irritably she switched on another tape, at full volume, so that the voices of Kirsten Flagstad and Svet Svanholm, singing the 'Liebestod' from *Tristan and Isolde*, obliterated the roar of the passing traffic. Then she turned it off. 'Oh, Christ!' The exclamation was audible to him as she got out of the car. For a while she stood over him as he fiddled with some wires. The vertebrae of his spine, each distinct, glistened with sweat. When he straightened and pressed a hand to the small of his back to ease a stiffness, she noticed the T of golden hair on his chest, also glistening with sweat. Appreciatively, she gazed at the swelling of his arm muscles as he tightened a screw.

'You seem to know what you're doing.'

He grunted something.

'Can you fix it, d'you think?'

'Yes, I think so. I hope so. I think one of the electric terminals must have worked loose.'

'How do you know about these things? Last month I was with a friend in his car, driving down to Brighton, and he couldn't even fix the puncture we had.'

'Well, I'm a mechanic by trade. Back home.'

'A *mechanic!*'

'Yep.'

'What on earth is a mechanic doing, travelling all over

Europe?'

'What everyone else is doing, I suppose.'

'A mechanic! Well, fancy that!'

As they made their way through the suburbs of Milan – he had a map on his knees, with her constantly prompting him with an impatient 'No, no, north of that, north!' or 'We're nowhere near that yet, miles and miles away!' – she said: 'We might as well see if we can get a room at the Astor Victoria. It's become a bit of a dump, terribly run down, but the people are nice and they know me – or, at least, always pretend they know me.'

'Oh, I couldn't stay in a hotel.'

'Why not?'

'Well, I couldn't afford it!' He laughed, throwing back his head. 'During all this trip I've never once stayed in a hotel. In fact, I've never stayed in a hotel in my life.'

'Where have you stayed?'

'In youth hostels. Mostly. Or in cheap rooming-houses. Or out of doors.'

'Aren't you a bit old for youth hostels?'

'Old?'

'Well, aren't they meant for schoolchildren, students, people of that sort of age?'

He shook his head. Then again he laughed. 'You find people of all ages in youth hostels. People older than me, older than you, much, much older.' She said nothing. 'Didn't you know that?'

'I am glad to say I've never set foot in a youth hostel.'

After seconds of frowning thought, he said: 'I think I'd better look for somewhere on my own.'

'Why?' she challenged.

'Well . . .' He could hardly say 'Because I don't want to share a room with you.' Again he hesitated. 'Because I don't like to be – beholden.'

'*Beholden!* What a wonderfully old-fashioned word!'

It was a word, he suddenly realised, that he had picked up from his father. He, too, did not like to be beholden and would often say so.

'I hate anything that brings an – an obligation.'

'Don't be silly. We'll get a room with two beds and we'll both sleep separately – a long, long night of uninterrupted sleep, after a long, long day of hard driving.'

He was silent.

'All right?'

'Yes. Okay. Thanks.'

She insisted on paying for the dinner in the cramped, expensive restaurant at which, as at the hotel, she was proud of being known. She had first been brought there, she boasted, by an Italian film-actor of whom, to her astonishment, Steve had never heard. 'Do refill our glasses,' she said at one point. 'That waiter seems determined to neglect us.' Then, in a voice which must have been audible to the diners around them, she cried out: 'No, no! Not to the brim, not to the brim! Where *were* you brought up?'

He laughed, taking no offence. 'In a Sydney slum where all anyone – with the exception of my Dad – ever drank was water or beer.'

Back in the hotel bedroom, he asked: 'Which of us do you want to undress first?'

'What do you mean? Can't we both undress at the same

time?' As she asked the second of these questions, her hand went to the top button of her blouse.

He turned his back to her as he began to strip off his shirt. Then, his back still to her, he sat on the bed which she had decided would be his, and began to unlace one of his heavy walking boots. He hoped, as when he had first clambered into the car, that there would be no smell from his feet or even his whole body. He had already showered once in the room, while she had gone off alone to see one of her Milan contacts, but the restaurant, so small and so crowded, had been hot even at the window table which she had demanded, and all through the meal he had been conscious of the damp spreading under his armpits and down his spine.

As though reading his thoughts, she said: 'You smell good, do you know that? Sometimes sweat, healthy sweat, can smell good.' He looked over his shoulder. She was standing at the end of the bed, in brassière and pants, her arms crossed over her large, firm breasts in a parody of modesty.

He looked away, saying nothing.

There was no lock to the door of the bathroom. He turned on the shower, first to warm, soaping himself vigorously under his armpits, in the crotch and across his swelling pectorals, and then to cold, relishing the sudden shock, which made him gasp repeatedly as though in an orgasm.

As he stepped out of the shower and reached for the towel, the door opened. She came in. She was totally naked. 'Oh! I seem to be too late to join you.' She put a hand to his chest and pressed him backwards until he could feel the tiles hard against his shoulder-blades and his buttocks. She knelt down on the bathmat before him, smiled up, lowered her head, so that her shoulder-length, brown hair, highlighted here and there with gold, screened her oval face.

He wanted to pull away. Then he realised that it was not unpleasurable. It was something that no one, not even Sue, had ever done to him before. He laid his head back, closed his eyes, caught his lower lip between his large, white, regular upper and lower teeth.

In Rome nothing happened prior to their going to sleep. But early in the morning he suddenly awoke, with a start and an incoherent exclamation, to the awareness that she had crept into his bed beside him. 'Not to worry, sugar. It's only me. I felt like a little cuddle.' He turned away from her with a muffled groan, pulling the sheet – it had been his only cover on an unusually hot and humid night – up to his chin. 'Oh, come on! Put your arms around me. Come on! I woke so early, feeling so depressed.'

Reluctantly he turned, put his arms around her, eventually held her close, closer. Her hand went down.

In Naples, they had been turned away from one restaurant – 'It's not only the most expensive but the best in the town,' she had told him – because Steve was not wearing a jacket or tie. They could supply both, the gross, amiable head waiter had said, if only *il signore* were wearing a shirt with a collar. The waiter said this in Italian and Irene then translated. Later, they had found a small fish restaurant with a balcony overlooking the sea. 'Let's go slumming,' Irene had said, pointing it out. 'Once when Boris and I were strapped for cash we went there and had some really delicious red mullet.' Steve did not know who Boris was. He had never eaten red mullet.

Staring down at the sluggish, greasy water, Steve said: 'I like it here. More my sort of place, much more. Let me shout you.'

'*Shout* me?'

'Treat you.'

'Certainly not. While you're with me, I pay. That's understood. I have my expenses, which I can easily fiddle. You have your – *budget.*' He had used that word in answer to her insistent questions about his finances. She managed to put it, as she so often managed to put words used by him, into mocking inverted commas. She mused for a moment. Then: '*Shout* me,' she repeated. 'What a quaint expression. I've never heard it before. It must be Australian.'

They drank one bottle and then another of a sharp, astringent wine – 'Far too cold,' Irene had said, putting a hand to the side of the first of the bottles, and then 'Oh, what the hell! What can one expect in a dump like this?' As she drank, so she became more and more amiable. For the first time she seemed to be actually interested in what, in his slow, drawling voice, he had to tell her. More than once she would say 'Oh, do tell me more about . . .', and would then ask him about his work at the garage or about his family or about the little house with the large garden, created by himself on an otherwise bare, barren suburban hillside, which he had sold in order to come on what he called 'my journey of a lifetime'.

When they left the restaurant, she overbalanced on the high, high heels of the elegant two-tone court-shoes – 'Ferragamo – bought in Florence on my last visit,' she had told him, as though he would know who Ferragamo was – staggered and clutched at his arm. He held her to him. He felt a sudden elation, followed by a no less sudden desire for her. Each emotion astonished him. When, in the hotel bedroom, before they had come out, she had put her arms around his neck and, standing on tiptoe, her lips to his, it was all he could do not to pull away. He now hugged her closer.

That night his bed remained empty. They slept glued to each other, his head on her bare breast, his mouth from time to time lazily seeking out her nipple, like a surfeited but still greedy baby.

After he had sat patiently in the car for over an hour, while she had seen a Palermo contact – 'there's not much point in seeing her, she seldom brings any business, the stuck-up old bitch, but I'd better make a try' – she marched, brief-case at the end of one arm and handbag under the other, down the marble steps, the colour of raw steak, and pulled open the door beside the driver's seat. He had repeatedly offered to take over the driving but she had replied, 'Oh, no, no, no! No, sweetie, that would *not* be a good idea. No one drives this car but yours truly.' She kicked off the Ferragamo shoes and then asked: 'Now where?'

'Where are you planning to go?'

'Back to England. *Tout de suite.*' She switched on the engine. 'Coming?'

He laughed. 'No. I told you. I've got to see Sicily. And then I want to move on to Greece. Maybe get a boat there.'

She sighed. 'Oh, well, that's probably just as well. You've

got a terrific body, not over-muscled but strong, strong, firm, firm, firm.' She leaned over and squeezed his right biceps. 'Just as I like a body to be. But frankly' – she gave a little laugh – 'you're not the most amusing company in the world, are you, sweetie?'

The car swung out from the kerb and, as it did so, the first drops of rain spattered down into the road. 'It looks as if you're going to get wet.'

'Yes.'

'Where would you like me to drop you? It can't be far from here because I want to catch that stinking ferry at seven twenty.'

'Anywhere. Anywhere at all. Here would be fine.'

He watched the car, the rain now sheeting down on him, as it veered off and away. He was preparing to wave to her. But she did not look round.

II

Stefano, his face oddly livid and his eyes glittering discs in the light from the brass lamp with the olive green shade on the desk beside him, looked up. '*Ecco!*' He reached for the cap of the old-fashioned, cigar-shaped, malachite fountain pen with which, tongue between teeth, he had been writing on a sheet of foolscap paper resting on a leather-bound blotter, and began to screw it on.

'I'm afraid I'm disturbing you.'

Stefano shook his head vigorously. 'All my life I have welcomed anything that disturbs me in my work. That's why, in sixty or so years, I've done so little.' He placed the pen on a rack on which two other equally old-fashioned pens, one purple and one gold, were slung horizontally. 'Have you settled in all right? That room is not too uncomfortable for you?'

'The room's fine. Far better than I'm used to! Yes, I've unpacked everything I have to unpack.' Steve amused fellow travellers in hostels by his tidiness. Each morning, before setting off on yet another leg of his odyssey, he would take out the whole contents of the backpack and then replace each item, one by one. Everything had its place. In the room which he had just left, the unsteady, eighteenth-century chest-of-drawers, painted with oranges on branches the green of which had faded to a silvery grey, already held his socks, T-shirts, underpants and handkerchiefs, all carefully segregated from each other.

'Bravo!' Stefano took up the sheet of paper before him, peered at it short-sightedly through his gold-rimmed glasses, and then slipped it into the top drawer of the desk. He jerked a key-ring from his trouser pocket and locked the drawer. Steve wondered why he should do so. Was there something on the sheet of paper which he wished no one else to see?

'Are you hungry, Steve?' It was the first time that Stefano had used the Christian name. He spoke it as though it were something odd, hesitating for a moment before coming out with it.

'Yep. I suppose I am! It's – oh – at least eight hours since I had anything to eat.'

'I heard my wife's patient leaving. At last! Even on the stairs he was telling her about one of his dreams. Just outside this door. No wonder I get so little written.'

Written? He must be a writer, Steve thought.

'I expect she's in the kitchen with Guido now. Then she'll call us and we'll go upstairs and, with luck, we shall have our dinner. Or, rather, supper. Dinner is altogether too grand for what we shall be having.'

Irene had laughed at Steve when, late in the evening, he had asked: 'Are we going to wait until we arrive in Rome to have our tea?' She had said: 'For me, tea is something which I have in the afternoon. If I have it. Which is seldom.'

'Are you a writer?' Steve now asked.

'Am I a writer? Well, I'm *trying* to be one. But, sadly, I've left it rather too late. Still . . .' He shrugged his narrow shoulders. Then, approaching Steve, he briefly put out a hand towards Steve's arm, without actually touching it.

'Don't be afraid of my wife. She is really very kind. And – and understanding. Her manner sometimes . . .' He gave an apologetic smile. 'I have explained about you. She will think of you as one of my stray dogs – that's what she calls people like yourself whom I try to help. But if you're a stray dog, then you're the sort of dog who would win a prize in any dog show. In any case, she loves any dog, even the ugliest mongrel . . . Have you ever thought – if you spell dog backwards, you get god?' He laughed and then, without waiting for an answer, went on in reassurance: 'She will like you.' He looked searchingly into Steve's face. 'I imagine that most people like you.'

Steve said nothing. On his last day at the garage, they had thrown a party for him. As he had stood, a mug of beer in one hand and in the other the brown envelope stuffed with the money collected for him, much to his embarrassment, as a farewell gift, he had been astonished and touched when one colleague after another had come up to him to tell him how much he would be missed. Then an elderly foreman, dwarfish, the deep-etched lines of his ill-natured face heavily ingrained with grease, his arms overlong and hairy, had strode over and barked: 'You know, Steve, I really hate you!' Steve had recoiled. It was something which he had always suspected, but it was odd of the foreman to put it into words now. Then the foreman went on: 'I hate you for quitting us like this. For Christ's sake, why d'you have to up stumps and fucking go?' At that, he had turned on his heel and strode off, long arms swinging.

From upstairs that deep, plangent voice called: 'Stefano! *Pronto! Vieni!*'

'Come!' Stefano put out a hand to the boy's back and

then withdrew it just as it was about to make contact.

Tilda, standing, legs astride, beside a trolley set out with dishes and plates, a serving spoon already in one hand, looked, with her immense height and her large, strong features, like some sergeant-major in the Grenadiers. She was wearing a shapeless pair of green corduroy trousers, gathered in at her narrow waist with a frayed leather belt with a brass snake for its buckle, and a man's long-sleeved, blue-and-white striped shirt, open at the collar, the sleeves fastened with elaborate silver cuff-links each showing what Steve was later to learn was the family crest of an eagle with a crown above it.

'This is my wife. She comes from not far from where your parents came from. Sweden. Tilda – this is Steve, of whom I've told you.'

Steve advanced, put out his hand. He did not often find people formidable. He found her formidable.

She squinted at him in a way which daunted him even more, the serving spoon still in her right hand. Her eyebrows were sparse above dark, brooding eyes.

'You are Steve,' she said in that deep, plangent voice.

'Yes. That's right.'

She put down the spoon, extended the hand. '*Molto piacere.*' She laughed: 'Do you know any Italian, Steve?'

He shook his head. 'Sorry.'

'I knew no Italian when I first came here more than thirty years ago. And I don't know much now. But I had an English nanny and so I speak English – nursery English.' In fact, having trained as an analyst in New York over a period of years, she spoke English almost as well as her husband, but with an American accent.

An old man in a white jacket, his back so curved that

he appeared to be perpetually scanning the ground for something, limped into the room carrying two bottles of wine, one red and one white, and a bottle of mineral water on a chipped, white plastic tray. He crossed over to the long mahogany table, its surface glistening under a chandelier, two of the six bulbs of which were dead. When Stefano spoke to him, he first placed the bottles carefully at the far end of the table and only then turned. With an attempt to straighten his body, he bowed and nodded to Steve in what was all too clearly no more than an ironic show of deference. He then gave his head a little shake and began to fiddle, mouth pursed, with the top of a silver salt-cellar, screwing it now this way and now that in hands twisted by arthritis, without ever being able to get it to fit properly.

'I have told him that you are our guest,' Stefano explained. 'After dinner, he can see to anything which you need for the room. I have told him that too.'

'Sit.' Tilda's voice was peremptory. She pointed to the chair between hers at one end of the table and Stefano's at the other. 'I'm afraid we're eating some warmed-up left-overs. My patient had so much to say, he stayed on and on. I hope you don't mind warmed-up left-overs?'

'That's fine by me. I'm so hungry I could eat anything.'

'Even the proverbial horse?' Stefano chuckled. 'When I lived in Bruges many, many years ago, I often ate horse. A delicacy.' He pulled back his chair.

'In Korea dog-meat is a delicacy.' Tilda made a face, striding back to the trolley where Guido, a plate held in two trembling hands, awaited her. What she now ladled out was some kind of tawny beef stew, its meat so tough and gristly that Steve thought that horse-meat or even dog-meat might have been preferable. To accompany it there was some lukewarm mashed potato and some roughly chopped courgettes, oozing not butter or oil but a greenish water.

When plates had been set down in all three places, Tilda drew back her chair and turned to Guido, who still stood, hands clasped before him, by the trolley.

'*Grazie*, Guido.'

'*Prego, principessa.*'

Steve, totally ignorant of Italian, did not then realise that his host and hostess were a prince and princess. He was only to learn it next day when, passing through the hall to his room, he glanced at the envelopes scattered across the massive chest which stood against one wall.

'Where are the dogs?' Stefano asked.

'I told Guido to shut them up in the kitchen. You know what they're like with a stranger. I don't want them yapping all through this meal. I'm too tired for it.'

'*Poveretti!*'

Tilda turned to Steve. 'Do you like dogs?'

'I've never owned a dog. But yes, yes, I like them.'

'Ours are the most beautiful dogs in the world,' Tilda said.

'And the noisiest. And the most bad-tempered. And the greediest,' Stefano took up.

'But we love them,' Tilda said.

Stefano sighed. 'Yes, we love them. Because we've nothing else to love. Except each other,' he added. Tilda frowned, as she struggled to slice into a chunk of meat with a knife the handle of which, like her ring, was embossed with the family crest. 'Do you know that I am the last of my line?' Stefano went on. 'Think of that! The family – the old, old family – will die out with me. And only a cousin is left of my mother's family. Tilda has a few relatives, but she never goes to Sweden and they never come here.'

'Which is just as well,' Tilda said.

To Steve the meal seemed interminable. He chewed on the meat and swallowed it with difficulty, while his host and hostess for the most part conversed not with him but with each other in a mixture of Italian, English and French. Steve gathered that Stefano had had some quarrel or at least an argument with an old friend about some land, that one of the dogs had worms, that one of Tilda's patients had tried to kill herself – 'That woman fails at everything she attempts. Of course she swallowed far too few pills,' was Tilda's rough verdict.

When either of the Italians addressed Steve, it was usually to interrogate him about Australia as though it were some obscure, impoverished Central African state from which he had only just emerged. Did any cities other than Sydney and Melbourne have airports, theatres, museums? Did many people watch television there? Had this new fashion for supermarkets taken on? Tilda even began to explain what a Vespa was.

At one point Stefano once again spoke of Patrick White. He had been born in Sydney, hadn't he?

'No, London,' Tilda corrected. 'What a dreadful character!' she added contemptuously. 'What a mess he's made of his life!'

'And what wonderful art he's made of the mess!' Stefano countered. He turned to Steve: 'Yes?'

Steve said nothing, merely raising a shoulder in its wrinkled T-shirt. Why hadn't it got through to them that he knew nothing about books, hardly ever read them, in fact had difficulty in reading a newspaper or writing all but the most simple and perfunctory of letters?

From the dining-table they moved into a small room, the only cosy and comfortable one, Steve was to discover, in the whole house, which Tilda used as her consulting room. It contained a *chaise-longue*, its pink damask badly frayed, where, Stefano was to explain on a later occasion, Tilda's patients lay out 'awaiting their torture', two huge armchairs covered in a chintz of a jazzy art deco design of interlocking triangles and quadrangles, a desk strewn with papers, a low Chinese-style table littered with books and magazines, and a cast-iron stove, unlit at this time of year, with a pipe which rose up from its rear, mounted the wall and then ran along a ceiling blackened by the leakage of smoke over innumerable winters. Guido brought in the coffee on the same chipped, white plastic tray on which he had previously brought in the bottles of wine and mineral water. He gave Steve a baleful sideways glance from under bushy white eyebrows. Did he resent the jeans, safari boots and T-shirt? Or did he resent having another person to serve? Perhaps both, Steve thought.

When his cup of coffee had been set down on the low table before him, Steve turned to his host. 'I hope' – he screwed up his eyes, trying in vain to recall Guido's name – 'I – I hope, er, er' – he indicated Guido – 'won't stay up. There's nothing I need for the present in my room.'

'Guido doesn't go to bed early. And he's too blind to read and too deaf to listen to the wireless,' Tilda said.

Steve laughed, embarrassed. 'Even so . . .'

At that moment feet thundered up the stairs and the

door was flung open. A tiny woman, with a shock of red hair and heavily mascaraed eyes, cried out: '*Ecco mi!*' as she rushed towards Stefano. He began to lever himself off the *chaise-longue*, muttering '*Cara, cara,*' but she pushed him back, while at the same time kissing him first on one cheek and then on the other. Now she rushed at Tilda, going down on her knees by her chair, throwing her arms around her and hugging her to her.

When all this was over, Tilda introduced Steve. 'This is Olive,' she said. 'My friend. My only friend, *real* friend. She comes from England. But she lived many years in Finland, with her first husband, and now she has lived many years in Italy. Olive speaks beautiful Italian, far better than mine. She also speaks beautiful Finnish – so Finns have often told me.'

Olive had jumped off the floor, as Steve had lumbered to his feet. She grasped his right hand in both of hers. She raised the hand to the level of her bony, seemingly breastless rib-cage. 'What a handsome young man!' she cried out. 'Who is he? Who is he?'

Stefano began to explain. Meanwhile, she stared, with her heavily mascaraed, bloodshot eyes, into his face, his hand still grasped in hers. 'How lucky you are to find such a handsome young man!' she exclaimed when Stefano had finished. 'Why do I never have such luck?'

'It's what's called serendipity,' Stefano said. It was a word which Steve had never heard before and was never to hear again. 'Serendip was the ancient name for Ceylon and there was this fairy-tale entitled *Three Princes of Serendip . . .*' His voice trailed off, as Olive, heedless, turned away from him to say something in a whisper to Tilda. The two women crossed over to the desk and Tilda began to hunt for something. Eventually she found it, jerking it up out of an accumulation of papers, unopened envelopes and scientific journals piled higgledy-piggledy. She said something to Olive and Olive emitted a squeal of laughter. They then bowed, their heads almost touching, over the paper in Tilda's hands.

'Olive and my wife run this animal charity. The first in Sicily, almost the first in the whole of Italy. In England the RSPCA has existed for many years. In your country also, I'm sure . . . But in Italy . . . Sometimes I cannot bear to think about the sufferings of animals in this country of ours. Diabolical!' Then he laughed: 'Which reminds me. The dogs! The dogs! They must be suffering now.'

He crossed over to the door, left ajar by Olive, and from the landing shouted to Guido to bring up the dogs. In a moment the three Pekineses had burst into the room, as precipitous as Olive. At once they rushed at Steve, yapping and nipping at him. '*Calma! Calma! Calma!*' Stefano pleaded, rather than ordered. The two women broke off their deliberation, and Tilda shouted in English: 'Quiet! Stop that! Stop!' The dogs fell silent. One, the smallest and most agile, managed with great difficulty to scrabble its way up on to the *chaise-longue* beside Stefano. One trotted over to the two women and stood beside them, squat legs wide apart and head raised and tilted to one side as though in interrogation. The third, tongue lolling out as it snuffled for breath, eventually stretched out at Steve's feet.

'Mimi likes you,' Stefano said. 'She is named,' he went on, 'after a great friend of ours, the wife of Guido Piovene. The writer,' he added, realising that the name had meant nothing to Steve. 'One of the greatest Italian writers of the century. Not that the Contessa is a bitch. Quite the contrary.' Once again Steve felt the urge to say: 'Look, I'm only a motor mechanic. I know nothing about writing and writers.'

Stefano and the two women now began to talk together in Italian. Steve lowered his hand – Christ, his nails were dirty, he suddenly realised, would they have noticed? – and began to stroke the head of the bitch at his feet, rhythmically, on and on, until the movement began to induce a trance not merely in her but in himself. Eventually, in a pause in the increasingly vehement conversation – so often in the future Stefano and Tilda would seem to him to be having a furious argument when in fact they were merely discussing something of no real importance to either of them – he got to his feet and said: 'Maybe I ought . . . Would you mind if I turned in?'

'Turned in?' The idiom clearly puzzled Stefano.

'He wants to go to bed,' Tilda said.

'Yes, the *poveretto* looks exhausted,' Olive said, smiling up at him to reveal small, irregular teeth smeared with lipstick. 'You must have been exhausting him with too much of your intellectual conversation. I myself know how exhausting that can be.'

'No, I'm just exhausted by too much travel. Days and days of it.'

'Well, now you must settle for a while,' Stefano said. 'Here with us. You can see Palermo from this house. I will show it to you.'

Until that moment Steve had thought that he was being put up only for the night.

III

The breakfast croissants, though warm, were dry in Steve's mouth and scattered fragments as he bit into them. The coffee was lukewarm and far more bitter than the instant coffee to which he was used. He and Stefano faced each other across the gate-leg table in the study, the three dogs now watching them intently and now snuffling for crumbs as they fell to the carpet.

'Today I am free. Or, rather, I shall make myself free. I ought to be working on my ridiculous book. But I prefer to give up this day to showing you my Palermo.'

'Oh, I'm sure I can find my own way around. If you have a map . . . Or I can buy one. I don't want to take up your time.'

'No, young man, I insist.' For the first time since Steve's arrival, Stefano looked happy, his eyes bright and his mouth no longer sagging in lines of disappointment. 'It's a beautiful day, as you've no doubt observed for yourself.'

'Yes, it is, isn't it?'

'What's the use of wasting a beautiful day on a book which will probably never get published or even finished?'

In the garage two cars stood side by side. One was a shabby little Fiat, with a buckled front bumper and a cracked front side-window on the driver's side. The other was a low-slung, open Bugatti, painted in two tones of garish yellow and mud brown, a gigantic wasp on wheels, which, Steve at once realised, dated from the early thirties. He rushed over to it.

'Is this still running?'

'Running? Running? No, I'm afraid it's stationary. Permanently stationary. We couldn't use it even before our driver left us.'

'Can't it be repaired?' Steve ran a hand over one of the highly arched rear mudguards, the caress leaving a smear in the dust.

Stefano shrugged. 'Perhaps. At great expense. But what would be the point? Petrol is so expensive.'

Even as his hand again rested on that high-arched rear mudguard, Steve was stung with the idea of getting the beautiful, expensive monster, a car more beautiful than any he had ever seen in the garage in which he worked or on the streets of Sydney, back on the road.

'Well . . .' Stefano said impatiently, walking over to the Fiat. '*Andiamo?* Shall we go?'

Reluctantly Steve sauntered towards him, from time to time glancing back at the Bugatti. 'Do you want me to drive?' he asked.

'Yes, yes, of course. If you don't mind. And if you have the right sort of licence.'

When Steve turned the key in the ignition, there was no response. Stefano struck his forehead with the heel of his hand. '*Idiota!* I forgot. I ought to have telephoned Beppo at the garage. There is something wrong with the engine.'

'Let's see if I can fix it.' Steve jumped out of the car, keys in hand, and hurried to its rear. When he had left the Sydney garage, long after midnight, after that raucous, boozy party to bid him farewell, he had said to the girl to whom he had offered a lift home: 'Well, it'll be at least six months before I get my hands dirty again.' Yet here he was about to fiddle with the engine of yet another car.

Stefano swung his legs out of the seat, rested his elbows on his knees, and then rested his chin on his palms. 'How can you fix it?' he eventually called out.

'I'm a mechanic back home.'

'A *mechanic!*' Stefano repeated the word with awe. 'I have so much admiration for people who can do things with their hands.' He now clambered out of the car and walked stiffly towards Steve. 'Have you ever thought what a wonderful thing the human hand is? A miracle of engineering! Yet the only thing of any value that I can do with my hands is hold a pen and write.' There was a pause. Then he said: 'Why are your hands so – so beautiful? You know, they were the first thing I noticed about you, as I passed that bench on which you were sitting in the rain. Those beautiful hands. Those are not a mechanic's hands. Those are the hands of a musician, an artist, a writer!'

Steve pulled a face and shrugged, still intent on examining the engine. 'My Dad has similar hands. Back in Lithuania he was studying to be a violinist. But usually my hands are grimy. They're like this because I haven't been working for some weeks.'

'Why did you never tell me that you were a mechanic?'

'You never asked me.' Steve turned his head and smiled at Stefano. Then he said: 'I think I see what's wrong.'

'Something serious?' Stefano might have been asking about the result of a life-or-death biopsy.

'No. I can fix it. I *think*.'

When, after some ten minutes, Steve had succeeded in fixing it, he switched on the ignition and, head to one side, listened to the engine.

'This engine needs retuning.'

'Retuning? That sounds as if you were talking about a piano.'

'Cars need retuning just like pianos,' Steve said. 'I'll see what I can do. But that'll be a long job. And I'll have to find the right tools. What you have in that tool-box of yours . . . Another time.'

'And you can really do this – this *retuning* for me?'

'Yes. That's my trade, isn't it? I'll be happy to do it in return for all your kindness to me.'

But he was really thinking of getting down to work, not on the tinny little Fiat, but on the Bugatti.

First they would go to the museum, Stefano said. Then he wanted to show Steve a house, a beautiful house, a palace in fact, no longer inhabited, the subject of a long and costly legal battle between himself and that distant cousin of his mother. Then . . . well, they would see.

Steve had never been into a museum since a far-distant occasion when, managing to slip away from the school party into which they were corralled, he and another boy, his only friend, slipped through a door which ought to have been locked and found themselves in the room of one of the curators. From a crumpled Gauloise packet left lying beside a typewriter, they had gleefully each extracted a cigarette. Sucking greedily at the pungent, pinched cylinder of paper, Steve had whirled himself on the merry-go-round of the curator's chair beside the typewriter, while his friend, legs swinging, had perched beside him on the desk. Then the door had flown open and a janitor, having smelled the smoke from the passage outside, had rushed in with a shout of 'Oi! What the bloody hell's going on in here?'

That night Steve's father, having been told of the delinquency by the headmaster of the school, had with slow deliberation taken off his belt and then ferociously thrashed the boy as he lay sprawled, face downwards, across the back of the sitting-room sofa. Meanwhile his mother, washing dishes at the sink, had pretended, as she always did, that nothing was going on.

Now, as Stefano conducted him from case to case, from picture to picture, from room to room, Steve was brooding on that one thrashing above all the innumerable others stretching back to his early childhood. He nodded from time to time but hardly listened, as Stefano pointed at now this object and now that, all the time intoning a lecture – there was no other way to describe it – which it seemed that he must have delivered many times before, so effortlessly did the words cascade from him. It was that thrashing which, at the age of eight, had decided Steve that as soon as possible he must quit home. But the actual quitting had come several years later.

Because of heavy rain, there had been a landslide which had delayed the bus journey from the centre of Sydney, where he had been attending a boxing match, to the shabby, sprawling near-slum in which he lived. His father had made the rule that he must always be home by eleven. Since the landslide had involved the bus in a lengthy detour, the fourteen-year-old boy had arrived at close on twelve. Having never been allowed a key of his own, Steve had rung the bell.

His father had pulled open the door, his pyjama jacket unbuttoned to reveal the thick mat of grey hair on his chest, and his small, red-rimmed eyes squinting with rage. Steve could smell the home-brewed wine on his breath. 'What time do you think this is?' The Lithuanian accent was thick even after all these years of exile. Steve began to explain about the landslide and the bus. Suddenly, he felt his father's fist slam into his face and, with the agony of the impact, also heard the crack of an eye-tooth. His father's knuckles began to ooze blood. 'If you can't fucking well get back in time, then you can't fucking well get in!' At that, his father again pulled back his short, muscular, hairy arm and, with all his force, slammed the door shut.

Steve stood before the closed door, hand pressed to mouth, in an attempt somehow to staunch the raging pain. Then he turned, stumbled off, paused to spit out a fragment of tooth and a strand of saliva and blood. As Stefano now said: 'This is an interesting Etruscan piece – not beautiful but interesting . . .', Steve again felt the combined nausea and rage which had filled him at that moment. He would never speak to his father again, never even see him again, he had vowed to himself, as he had begun the long trek to the house of his married sister, on the other side of the city.

Suddenly Stefano said, in a tenderly solicitous voice, his eyes searching Steve's face: 'You are bored. Poor boy – you are bored.'

'No. No, not at all. It's just . . .' He had no wish to hurt the old man's feelings. 'It's just that . . . I slept badly last night. I'm a little tired. And I was – I was also – thinking of something . . .'

'Yes, going round a museum can be a tiring business. It requires so much concentration. Let's go. But before we go, I must just show you . . . Come! Come! Please!' He moved away, then turned, beckoned. 'This is something truly beautiful.'

The two men stood side by side, as the older said in what was almost a whisper: 'This is what we call Capodimonte. You have heard of Capodimonte?'

'Sorry. I'm terribly ignorant, you know.' Steve gave a nervous, self-deprecatory little laugh, such as was often to be his response to incomprehensible or bewildering things said to him by the old man.

'You poor boy!' Stefano said not in mockery but in genuine concern. 'It's one of the most beautiful of all soft-paste porcelains. This figure represents – well, you can see for yourself – a shepherd with a sheep. It was probably modelled by Stefano Gricci. There are some Capodimonte figures in my study, you may have seen them. But none is as – as exquisite as this.' He sighed deeply, then turned away.

Steve continued to stare at the figure, and for a brief moment he shared in the old man's pleasure in it. Then he again remembered, trying in vain to exorcise the image, his father's congested face, the squinting, red-rimmed eyes, the fist smashing into his mouth. He turned away. It was impossible that this old man, shuffling ahead of him, could ever have made such an attack on anyone, let alone his own son, in the whole of his life; and, as he thought that, he all at once experienced a feeling of gratitude and, yes, tenderness.

Stefano now halted before a fresco. He tilted up his head on its short neck and, mouth pursed, stared at it. Steve waited patiently beside him, his eyes not on the fresco but on the lozenge pattern of red and green tiles on the floor. 'This dates from the fifteenth century. Originally painted for the Palazzo Scalafani, which then belonged to some ancestors of mine. It's called *The Triumph of Death.*'

Now Steve looked at the fresco. Death was a skeletal archer on an emaciated horse. Stefano raised a hand, pointed. 'Your arrow won't get you for a long, long time. But mine . . .' He turned away. 'You like it?'

How could one like anything so morbid and depressing? But Steve felt obliged to say, 'Yes, I like it.'

'I will teach you to like such things. You are an intelligent boy, I can see that. You will learn quickly.' Then he put out a hand and all but touched Steve's shoulder. 'I had planned to take you on to Santa Maria degli Angeli. There are some wonderful stuccoes there by Giacomo Serpotta. But I think that you have had enough of such things for the day. Yes?' Steve nodded reluctantly. 'So – *andiamo!*' Again, like a butterfly skimming a branch, the hand all but alighted on Steve's shoulder.

Steve enjoyed the feeling of mastery as he coaxed the reluctant, gasping little vehicle up one incline and then up one even steeper. Looking for a moment over his shoulder, he saw the city far, far below. In the heat that was already intense at that hour of the morning, its buildings seemed to be smouldering, as trails of vapour wriggled aslant from them and then drifted upwards. A similar conflagration seemed to have scorched to the colour of putty the vegetation on either side of the steep, narrow, unmade road.

Stefano leaned forward and from the glove compartment in front of him drew out a fan. He clicked it open, to reveal a design, in a few bold, simple strokes, of a stork beside a stream, with the branch of a willow tree drooping above it. 'A present from a Japanese writer. He visited me. We had an interesting silence together.' He smiled. Then he raised the fan and gently swayed it back and forth before his face.

'Hot,' he said. 'But I love this heat. I feel at my best in it. You know, I awoke at five this morning and was working on my novel at half-past five.'

'Is it going well?'

Stefano shrugged. '*Chi lo sa?*' Then, realising that Steve could not have understood him: 'Who knows?' At that, smiling, he leaned across and flapped the fan back and forth beside Steve's cheek.

Steve laughed. 'If you do that, I might drive us both off the road!'

Stefano jerked his body upright and away. After a few moments of staring ahead of him, he folded the fan and, gripping it tightly in both hands, rested it in his lap. Spots of red had appeared in his sallow cheeks. Steve wondered if he had upset him. But how could he have done so with so obviously playful a remark?

Steve turned, at Stefano's direction, off the road into a drive even rougher. Branches from the straggly trees arching above made a rasping noise as they scraped the roof of the car. Each pot-hole or rut caused Stefano's body to tip over now towards Steve and now towards the window. A brown mane of grass, flattened here and there

by previous vehicles, bristled up the centre of the drive.
At one moment a huge, shaggy dog – of a kind used for
hunting in Sicily, Stefano explained – shot out of the
undergrowth, barking its displeasure.

'Here! Here! Turn left – no, right, right! And here –
here stop before that *villetta*, that little house. Yes, yes,
here, here!' Later Steve was to notice that the old man
often had difficulty in differentiating between right and
left. But when, on one occasion, he had jokingly
suggested that he should have L and R tattooed on the
backs of his hands, Stefano had bunched his mouth,
drawing down its corners, in obvious affront.

As the car drew up before the *villetta*, the massive dog,
still barking, loped up beside it. 'Do you think it safe to
get out?' Steve asked. As a child, he had once been badly
bitten by a neighbour's German Shepherd. In his calf he
still bore the deep, jagged indentation. His mother had
wanted to take him to hospital to have the almost
bloodless wound stitched up, but his father had scoffed
that that wasn't necessary, it was nothing, as usual the boy
was making a fuss to get attention, all that was necessary
was to disinfect it and it would heal on its own.

'Oh, yes. Yes. He's called Bruno. He is barking only to
welcome us.' Stefano opened the door on his side and
swung out his legs. The dog raced round the car and
jumped up at him as he emerged. Stefano lowered a
hand and placed it on the dog's head. '*Bene, bene, bene!*' he
crooned. After a moment the dog unfurled a huge
tongue and wrapped it around the old man's wrist. 'You
see! He is very friendly.'

But Steve, now emerging from the car, still felt nervous;
and this nervousness intensified when the dog, once

again racing around the car, lowered its grizzled muzzle to his ankles and began to growl.

'Bruno! *Basta! Basta!*'

Eventually the dog sloped off to the shade of an olive tree, where it stretched itself out and at once fell asleep.

'Knock!' Stefano ordered, pointing at the door of the *villetta*. He was used to giving orders; his voice, usually so gentle, often acquired, as on this occasion, a peremptory edge when he did so.

Steve raised the knocker and let it clatter down.

'Again! There must be someone there.'

Once more, Steve raised the knocker.

There was a sound from behind the door of someone walking heavily towards it. Then a huge, unshaven man, with a broken nose, a scar over an eyebrow and gaps between yellow, uneven teeth, was standing before them, in a check shirt torn under an arm, baggy, dark blue trousers and slippers. When he saw Stefano, his previously hostile expression changed to one of welcome. '*Principe! Benarrivato!*'

Stefano extended both his hands and the man grasped them, by the wrists, in his. In those loud, vibrant, rapid Italian tones, which always suggested to Steve that a quarrel or at least something exciting must be afoot, the two men conversed for a while. At one point Stefano put an arm around the other man's shoulders and hugged him to him. Steve always shrank from any human contact, except when making love – 'You're not exactly a *tactile* person, are you?' Irene had reproached him on one occasion, when he had patently squirmed away from the hand which she had placed on his shoulder. He had not known what the word 'tactile' meant but was too embarrassed to ask. With Stefano he was never to feel a similar embarrassment. 'I'm sorry, I've no idea what that word means,' he would say, and patiently the old man would explain to him.

Already used to the deferential way in which everyone other than Tilda and Olive treated Stefano, Steve was amazed by the matiness of this unkempt, middle-aged man in his torn, dirty clothes towards the head of the aristocratic house which presumably employed him. Stefano might have been his equal, a friend, even his father or an elder brother.

Now Stefano turned to Steve. 'I am sorry, Steve, I am sorry! I am being very rude. I am talking to Marco and ignoring you.' He said something in Italian to Marco, and Marco thrust out a huge hand, the palm of which was hard and scaly to the touch. '*Molto piacere, signore.*'

Steve mumbled: 'Glad to meet you,' and gave his slow, shy smile, lids slightly lowered over downcast eyes.

The two Italians chattered to each other, Marco's arm around Stefano's shoulder, as they sauntered along a path, through the red marble chips of which weeds had long since thrust their way. The sun, now almost overhead, beat down on Stefano's ancient panama hat with its wide red-and-white ribbon, and on Marco's tonsure-like bald patch and the thick, grey curls impinging on it. Steve was a step behind them. For a brief time the dog was behind Steve, making him wonder fearfully whether at any moment, now, even now, it might not tear at his calf with its fangs. Then it gave up and once more retreated to the shade of the olive tree, where, desultorily, it began first to scratch and then to snuffle for fleas.

As the huge, crumbling palace, previously all but concealed by overgrown trees, came into view, Stefano halted and turned. 'That façade is almost the equal of Versailles, isn't it?' Then, seeing Steve frown: 'Or perhaps you've never been to Versailles.'

Steve shook his head. 'Someone told me I ought to go when I spent my three days in Paris. But there was so much else to see. One can't see everything, can one?'

'You are absolutely right. One can't.' Stefano gave that sweet, slightly sorrowful smile of his. Then he began, in that lecturer's voice which Steve was so much to dread in the days to come: 'The building of this palace was begun at the outset of the seventeenth century by Antonino Amato. He also designed the church of San Niccolo in the Piazza Dante in Catania. We must go together to Catania. There is so much to see there. There are so many places in Sicily to which we must go together.'

At the words, Steve suffered a shrivelling of the spirits. Time after time on this 'journey of a lifetime' he had rejected invitations from fellow travellers, usually met in youth hostels, that he should join up with them. 'Sorry,' he would say. 'Thank you. But I'm afraid I'm a loner.' He had been schooled in that fierce independence in his youth. His family, partly because it was the only immigrant one in the neighbourhood and partly because of the quarrelsomeness of its head, had suffered an almost general ostracism. Many of the local children were openly hostile to Steve and his sister. Many more refused to allow them to join in their activities. Of most of the meagre rest, their father forbade them to have contact with all but half a dozen – the others came of 'bad' families, he would say, their mothers were 'little better than tarts', their fathers were 'scum'.

Inside the first courtyard, Stefano tilted his head upwards and rotated himself on his small feet in their black, patent-leather moccasins, to survey the crumbling building. 'Sad, sad,' he muttered. 'I can remember this palace . . . In my novel, I write of it as it was in its days of glory – with its hunting parties, its card parties, its amateur theatricals, its balls.' Later, in one of a series of vast *saloni* – 'I think that one can safely say that this is the most flamboyant rococo decoration in the whole of Sicily' – he pointed at a ceremonial bed in a niche at its furthest end. 'That is where the princesses of the house – distant ancestors of mine – would receive their visitors while still recovering from producing their innumerable children. Children died easily then. So it was essential to keep up the supply.' He sighed and pulled a rueful grimace. 'I'm afraid I've broken that tradition. The supply has run out.'

As they trudged down long, vaulted passages, echoing with the scrape and clatter of their feet, mounted sweeping staircases, the corners of their marble treads clogged with the dust of years, or passed from one room with damp, peeling walls, to another crammed with broken furniture, the chairs covered in tattered damask and the buhl of the tables long since sprung, Steve felt a depression and weariness descend on him. On and on Stefano lectured, while Marco, a ring of vast, rusty keys dangling from a forefinger, stood beside him, his face expressing a resigned passivity. Steve longed to move from this gloom and dust, from these peeling, damp-stained walls, from these immensely high ceilings, back into the sunshine and the heat. He thought of the hills behind the palace and of walking up and up one of them, with his pack on his back, and nothing to which to listen but the wind in the trees and the songs of the birds.

At long last, they emerged, not from the front of the house but from its rear, into a courtyard surrounded by what had once been the stables and the carriage-houses. In one of the carriage-houses there was still an ancient brougham, its mahogany chipped and scratched and one of its four wheels missing, so that it rested at a tilt. 'That came from England,' Stefano said. 'My great-grandfather brought it from England. As a child I remember riding in it.'

Marco said something and Stefano then translated: 'Marco invites us for a cup of coffee – or a grappa, if you prefer.' Steve had no idea what a grappa was. 'The grappa is from the estate,' Stefano added, as Steve hesitated as to what to reply.

Steve scrabbled for his courage. 'What I'd really like to do is have a walk. Up there!' All at once he had glimpsed a classical pavilion glimmering out of the olive green of the trees on the hillside ahead of him.

'A walk! In this heat! No, no, you'd do far better to come into the little courtyard behind the *villetta* and rest for a while.'

Steve laughed. 'I don't need a *rest!* But I'd love some fresh air and some exercise.'

Stefano pursed his lips and all but closed his eyes. 'Very well. As you wish. When you have had your *little walk*' – he gave a scathing emphasis to the two words – 'then you can knock on the door of the *villetta*. Yes?'

Steve nodded. He knew, as he walked away, that he had offended the old man; but as he mounted higher and higher up the hill and the air became fresher and fresher, he cared less and less. When a glance at his watch showed that he had already been away for more than half an hour, he resisted the temptation to turn back and instead strode at an even faster pace up towards the temple.

The temple itself, half of its pediment broken off and its interior full of ordure and soiled scraps of newspaper – no doubt the labourers used it as a lavatory – was far from alluring. So, instead of entering it to rest for a moment on one of its marble benches, Steve perched on the trunk of a tree which must have been blown down in a gale. He gazed out over the feathery tops of the trees to the sea. A large ship, its single funnel belching a purple-grey smoke, was gliding from one side of the tranquil bay to the other, incising its wake as with a chisel. All at once he was filled with the desire to be on that ship, moving on, on, on. As a boy in Sydney he would feel that same desire as at night, far off from his home, he would hear unseen trains thundering down and then receding, until the only sound from them was no more than a faint exhalation, like the sigh of a far-off wind.

The two men were drinking wine, Marco perched on a straight-backed chair turned the wrong way round, his hands clasped around it when he was not raising his glass to his lips, and Stefano half-reclined on two cushions placed on a wrought-iron bench. The sunlight struck fire from the carafe between them. It glowed, a furnace red. Once again they gave the impression not of superior and inferior but of long-standing friends.

'*Eccolo!*' Stefano cried out as he saw Steve. He raised his glass in salutation and then drank from it. He was clearly happy, even joyful; any hurt at being abandoned had been forgotten. He made a space for Steve on the bench, patting it. Then he tugged out one of the cushions from under him and, despite Steve's protests, placed it on the space. Steve lowered himself.

Stefano reached for the glass which rested, unused, on a metal tray. 'You will try some of this wine?'

Steve shook his head. 'Thank you. I'm – I'm not really all that fond of wine. Now if there was some beer . . .'

'It's no use coming to Italy if you're not really all that fond of wine.' Then he relented. 'But never mind . . . Perhaps Marco can produce . . .' He turned to Marco and said something in Italian. Marco grinned, shook his head. 'I'm afraid not. Sorry.'

'Actually, what I'd really appreciate is some water. Just some water. That walk in the heat made me thirsty. And my throat still seems full of dust after our time in the house – the palace,' he quickly corrected himself.

'Well, I'm sure that *water* is something that Marco can find for you. But whether he can also find ice . . .'

'Oh, I don't need any ice. Just water. Water will be fine.'

As Marco shambled off, Steve for the first time became aware of a young woman standing motionless at a ground-floor window to one side of him. She was wearing a black dress and a black cloth was wound round her head. She was staring out intently, her face wary, even hostile, her hands resting on the sill. He thought: Christ, she's beautiful! When their eyes met, it was his, not hers, which eventually looked away, so unnerving was the fixedness of her gaze. Was she Marco's wife? His daughter? A servant?

As Steve raised the glass of water to his lips, Stefano peered frowningly at the young man's arm, its blond hairs glinting in the sunlight, as though something about it puzzled him. Then he said: 'You're very sunburned.'

'Yes, I know.' Now Steve, having set down the glass, gazed at the arm too. 'When my sister and I were very small, my mother used to put us out in the sun. That wasn't such a good idea. Last year my sister had to have a melanoma removed. There's a lot of melanoma in our country now.'

'This is a new idea, that the sun is bad for one. When I was sent to Switzerland with tuberculosis, part of my treatment was to lie out in a balcony in the sun.' As though the word tuberculosis had somehow precipitated it, Stefano was all at once convulsed with coughing. On and on he went, one hand pressed to his breastbone, while the tears sprang to his eyes and began to trickle down his cheeks. '*Maledetto!*' he gasped; and then, in a choked voice, as though some invisible hand were tightening round his throat, 'Damn, damn, damn!'

'Are you all right?'

Marco had risen to his feet. Now he reached for Steve's half-finished glass of water and held it, with a surprisingly tender concern, to Stefano's lips, his other hand on his shoulder. Still coughing, Stefano took a small sip and then a longer one. '*Grazie! Grazie mille!*' He could hardly get the words out, as, eyes glistening with tears, he smiled up at Marco in gratitude.

'Are you all right?' Steve repeated.

'As all right as I am ever likely to be,' Stefano croaked. 'If only you could retune my body as you plan to retune the Fiat!' He gave Steve the same weak smile which he had just given Marco and tweaked out of the breast pocket of his grey raw-silk suit a large handkerchief with his initials, surmounted by a crown, embroidered on it in black thread. He pressed the handkerchief first to one eye and then the other. 'My chest has always been weak. Even as a child. Friar's balsam, you know friar's balsam? My English nanny – Miss Pringle – was constantly, constantly making me inhale it.' He shuddered. 'Horrible smell!'

When they eventually got up to go, Steve at first wondered whether Stefano had drunk too much of the wine, so erratically did he walk, lurching from side to side. Then he decided that the coughing fit must in some way have affected his balance. He extended an arm: 'Can I help you?'

'Help me? How do you mean?' The tone was sharp.

Steve said nothing more.

As they began to take one hairpin bend after another in their descent, Stefano turned to ask: 'What did you think of Marco?'

Steve shrugged. 'How can I have any opinion? We didn't talk. I couldn't understand a word he was saying.'

'He's a good soul. Kind. Reliable.' He thought for a moment: 'The people that I like most are intelligent, not intellectual. Like Marco. Like you,' he added, turning his head to smile at Steve. 'Marco and I are close, always close – ever since he was just a young boy. And yet. . .' He drew a deep sigh, which brought on yet another, less severe fit of coughing. 'And yet . . . he is a Mafia assassin. Yes, yes.' He nodded his head vigorously, as though Steve had contradicted this verdict. 'I assure you, I assure you! That tells you something about this Sicily of ours. I know that Marco is a Mafia assassin and everyone in this neighbourhood knows. None of us will ever tell the police, because the police also know. For generations my family ruled a large area of Sicily, but we do nothing about a Mafia assassin, we even employ him. And I am – well – his protector.' He gave a dry, humourless laugh, his body shaking with it, as it had previously shaken with the coughing. 'Can you imagine? Such a thing would be impossible in Australia, I think.'

'In Australia we don't have ruling families, to begin with.'

'And you don't have a Mafia!'

'Well, no, not exactly.'

Again Stefano emitted that dry, humourless laugh, which seemed to crepitate somewhere deep inside him. Then, head tilted to one side, he stared down in appraisal of Steve's boots. Eventually he said: 'How can you bear to wear such boots on a day as hot as this?'

'Well, it was either them or my sandals. I have nothing else. Actually, they're very comfortable. Wonderful for trekking. The leather is soft, you wouldn't believe how soft. I brought them from Australia with me. They were very expensive. A goodbye present from my mother.'

Again Stefano tilted his head and looked down at the boots. He frowned. 'They are not very elegant.'

'I didn't choose them because I thought they were elegant. I chose them because they were comfortable and would last a long time.'

'But you must be so hot in them, poor boy!'

'I'm used to them. They breathe quite well, you know.'

'Breathe! *Breathe?* Stefano pulled a face. 'Do shoes breathe? Are they living things?' Then he said: 'I have an idea. Before we eat, we will go to Ferrucci.'

'Ferrucci?'

'Where the most elegant shoes in Sicily can be found.'

'But I don't want any shoes. They'd only be one more thing to carry.'

'When you leave Palermo, I can get Guido to post them to you in Sydney, if you don't want to take them with you.'

'In any case my budget doesn't stretch to a new pair of shoes.'

'Maybe not. But mine does.'

'Oh, I couldn't possibly . . .'

'Why not? Your presence has given me so much pleasure already. You know, these days there is not much pleasure in my life. So why should I not make you some return?'

'But I hate to be beholden.'

'*Beholden?*' Like Irene before him, Stefano repeated the word in mockery.

'I loathe any obligation.'

'But there *is* no obligation. I told you. You have given me something and now I wish to give you something. Is that so strange?' Frowning over the wheel at the road ahead, Steve did not answer. 'Is it?'

Steve shook his head, said nothing. He felt confused, anxious, pleased, somehow threatened. He wanted to be out of the car, away from Stefano, out on the road by himself; and yet at the same time he felt that tenderness which, once before that same day, had taken him by surprise, and had not been wholly welcome, since somehow, in some way, he felt that it unmanned and weakened him.

'Those are the shoes for you. Believe me! They are elegant, they are strong, they are light. They are perfect for the summer.' Stefano turned to the salesman with the tight jacket and trousers and the quiff of upbrushed greying hair and said something in Italian. The salesman nodded his head vigorously and said: '*Si, si, è vero, principe.*'

'You see – he agrees with me.'

Steve pushed a hand into the shoe not on his foot, held it to the light streaming through the window beside him, and turned it this way and that, examining it with a frown of concentration. He shook his head. 'No. Not for me.'

'What is wrong with them?'

'I've never worn shoes like that. They're – they're just *not me.*'

'If you've never worn shoes like that, then it's about time you did,' Stefano said tartly.

'Anyway, they're terribly expensive.'

'What has the expense to do with you? These shoes are a present from me. A *present!* Don't you understand?'

'Yes, I know. But . . .'

Unhappily, Steve once again turned the shoe this way and that on his hand, peering at it closely, as though for some defect.

'There is no but. You won't find better shoes anywhere in Italy – anywhere in the world. You know that the best shoes are Italian, don't you? Greta Garbo, Marlene Dietrich, Cary Grant, Tony Curtis, Ginger Rogers – all the great stars buy their shoes in Italy. Once I saw Garbo here in Ferrucci. The Onassis yacht was anchored in the bay and she made a special journey.'

Steve heaved a deep sigh.

'Steve, we will take them! You will wear them now. And this young man will wrap up those horrible boots for you.'

'But I honestly don't . . .'

'Please do not argue.' Stefano's tone was imperious. He might have added: 'I'm not used to people arguing with me.' He turned to the assistant, at the same time drawing a worn crocodile-skin wallet out of the breast pocket of his jacket. As he counted out the notes, he said: 'You will never regret owning such shoes. All your friends in Australia will admire them and covet them. I promise! They will last for ever! – or, at least, longer than I will last.'

Steve shrugged; then, shoes scattered around the spindly gold-painted chair on which he was seated, he looked up at Stefano to give him a rueful smile. 'Thank you. Thank you very much.'

In the car, Stefano, who had appeared to be lost in thought, suddenly said: 'What you don't understand is that giving can be a pleasure. More than receiving. Christ said that it is better to give than to receive. He should have said not better but more enjoyable. I hope that you are happy to have been given such beautiful shoes. But you cannot possibly be as happy as I am to have given them to you.'

'I don't understand . . . Why should you . . .?'

'Why should I what?'

'You hardly know me.'

'I feel I know you very well. It's as though you were someone I've known all along. Someone who, a long time ago, disappeared from my life and then, after many, many years, returned, returned totally unchanged. *È strano ma è vero.*'

Stefano had said that he was going to take Steve to his club; but then, realising that Steve's T-shirt and jeans

would not be acceptable, he decided on a change of plan.
'I have another idea. You will find the club very boring –
one old man like me is enough, you do not want a crowd
of them. Let's go to the Palumbo d'Oro.' As twice before
that morning, he all but put a hand on Steve's shoulder,
then at the last moment withdrew it. 'Turn first right
here. Then take the next right. The Palumbo d'Oro is
one of the oldest restaurants in Palermo. Also one of the
best.'

'Oh, don't spend too much money. You've spent so
much on those shoes.' As he had been driving, Steve had,
with difficulty, converted the lire for the shoes into
Australian dollars and had then been appalled. In Sydney
he could have bought at least four pairs of shoes for that
price.

'I want you to have nothing but the best.'

Steve laughed, taking it as a joke. 'But why, why? I'm
not used to the best, I've never had it in my life.'

'You have yourself given the answer to your question.'

The *maître d'hôtel* abandoned two elderly American
tourists with whom he had been dealing and rushed
forward to greet Stefano. He bowed comically low as he
did so. Then he waved an arm in the direction of the
window, where a long table had been set out for six. Was
Stefano expecting a party? Steve wondered. But soon he
realised that this table was for the two of them alone.

'What would you like to eat?'

Steve stared at the menu. He understood none of it.
'This is all Greek to me. Or, rather, Italian!'

'Let me translate.'

Painstakingly Stefano began to do so, until Steve

interrupted him: 'Why don't I just have what you have?'

Stefano smiled across, lowering the menu. 'Because in that case you would have very little. And I'm sure that after that walk of yours up into the hills you must be hungry. But, if you really wish it, then I will order for you, Yes? Do you really wish it?"

'Yes, I really wish it.' Steve laughed. 'Please.'

Stefano spent a long time on his choices. Steve had probably never eaten polenta, had he? He might not like it, a lot of foreigners didn't. Perhaps a *pasta alle vongole* would be better? For a second course how about the *quazzetto di lepre* – the jugged hare? The restaurant was noted for it. Or, of course, there were the usual veal dishes. Did Steve share the ridiculous repugnance to veal so common now among the Anglo-Saxon peoples?

Finally, Stefano picked up the wine list. 'There's a wine which I particularly like, called Corvo. I think that one of the reasons I like it so much is that Corvo was the name taken by that very *odd* English writer called Frederick Rolfe. *Baron* Corvo was what he liked to call himself – though he was no nearer to being a Baron than you are.' Then he remembered: 'Oh, but of course, you don't drink wine. You'd like some beer, wouldn't you?'

'Yes. That's what I'd really like in this heat. I'm very thirsty.'

Soon the restaurant was full, with a number of people waiting for tables to be vacated. But the *maître d'hôtel* never suggested that anyone else should sit at their table for six, even though he was now packing the other larger tables dotted about the restaurant with customers who, in many cases, were strangers to each other.

Suddenly, among the people standing impatiently by

the entrance, Steve saw a diminutive man in check trousers and a matching jacket which buttoned almost to the huge polka-dot bow tie nestling under his long, pointed chin. He had a number of books tucked beneath an arm. His sparse hair was a curious shade, the colour of tomato ketchup, and his cheeks had a floury look, as though they had been powdered.

Suddenly this man's darting eyes alighted on the table in the embrasure by the window. He rushed forward. 'Stefano! *Caro!*' He held out his arms; but Stefano, though he rose to his feet, did not throw himself into them. Instead, after delivering a perfunctory greeting, he turned to Steve: 'This is Sicily's leading playwright.' He said a long name, immediately lost on Steve. There followed some words in Italian to the playwright, who put out his hand. Steve, who by now had got to his feet, grasped it with his usual firmness. The playwright let out a little squeak. '*Ma come è forte, il Suo amico!*' He rubbed the back of the hand with the fingers of the other, as though attempting to chafe warmth into it, at the same time pulling a wry face.

Stefano had clearly been put out when the playwright had asked if he might sit with them and had only grudgingly acquiesced. But now he seemed determined to entertain the newcomer, talking volubly now in Italian and now in English and throwing back his head to laugh, as frequently at something which he himself had said as at something said by his friend.

The waiter attending to them was a handsome youth with over-large, peasant hands and a sulky expression. As he set down a basket of bread, the playwright watched him intently. Then, just as the boy was moving off, he put some question to him, to receive the muttered answer '*Da Napoli, signore.*'

'He is from Naples,' the playwright leaned forward to tell Steve across the table. 'He is new in this place. I see him now for the first time.'

Stefano's mouth was pursed. He gazed out across the room, over Steve's head, raised his glass of wine and sipped from it, sipped from it again. Suddenly he had become stiff and silent. Steve knew that something had upset him.

Each time that the waiter came to the table, the playwright had something to say to him. A lock of that strange, sparse, tomato-ketchup-coloured hair flopping over a forehead in the deep corrugations of which beads of sweat glistened, he would wriggle and giggle, his voice from time to time shooting up an octave. With impassive politeness the waiter would answer him.

At one moment during this badinage, Stefano leaned forward and hissed something in Italian. The playwright laughed, then put out his tongue.

When not flirting with the waiter, the playwright attempted to carry on a conversation with Steve, since Stefano was all too clearly not disposed to talk any longer. How old was Steve? Was he married? Did he have a girl-friend? Didn't Italian girls fall instantly for someone so handsome? As the questions became more and more intrusive, so Steve became more and more embarrassed. He realised that, just as the playwright had been flirting with the waiter, so now he was flirting with him.

The waiter returned with their coffee, served not as Steve liked it, with milk in large cups, but black and bitter in minuscule ones. The playwright once more leaned forward, the tomato-ketchup-coloured lock of hair again flopping over the sweat-beaded forehead. '*Sa qualquecosa?*' he asked the waiter. '*Le i è bello, molto bello.*'

Suddenly the legs of Stefano's chair screeched across the marble floor. He flung down his napkin. His face had become extraordinarily pale. 'Steve! We are leaving! Come! Come!' He began to cough, to cough more and more violently, the extraordinarily pale face now becoming extraordinarily red.

The playwright half rose, put a hand on his arm to restrain him, said something in remonstration. Stefano jerked away from him. 'Steve!'

Steve followed the old man out towards the reception area. What had the playwright said to arouse him to so much fury?

When they were once more in the car, Steve placed the key in the ignition and then said: 'Something upset you.'

Stefano did not answer.

'Something upset you,' Steve repeated.

Still silent, Stefano stared out stonily ahead of him.

When they entered the palace, Tilda called down in that deep, vibrant voice of hers: '*Stefano — è tu?*'

'*Si, si, cara!*' the old man called back, removing his panama hat and placing it and his slim, gold-knobbed stick on the chest still littered with unopened letters.

Tilda now appeared on the staircase, the three Pekineses, heads cocked, behind her. She was wearing what might have been a man's pale grey suit, the tightness of its trousers emphasising the swelling contours of her buttocks, and a mauve silk shirt with a flopping cravat of a darker mauve. What had become of them? she demanded. She and Olive had waited for them until almost two. It was really too bad, so inconsiderate not to have given her any warning when they went out or at least to have telephoned. All this she said in English, not Italian, clearly wishing not merely Stefano but also Steve to be aware of her displeasure.

Stefano rushed to her, putting his arms around her and then his head on her chest. A stream of Italian poured out of him. With Steve his manner and tone were both so often imperious; now with Tilda they were placatory, submissive.

After a short while, Tilda in effect shrugged him off. 'Olive is still here. Come and have some coffee with us.'

Stefano hesitated. 'I thought of a siesta . . .' Then seeing Tilda's face beginning to darken with renewed displeasure, he went on: 'But some coffee – why not? What could be more welcome?' He turned to Steve. 'Some coffee?'

Steve could still taste the restaurant espresso disagreeably bitter on his tongue. But, not wishing to cause any more offence to Tilda, he nodded and said: 'Thank you, that would be nice.'

Tilda led the way up to a storey above the one on which Guido had served them their coffee on the evening before.

They passed through a room empty but for three straight-backed, bentwood chairs standing in a line against one wall, and a wicker dog-basket in a corner, and out on to a narrow balcony, shaded by a striped canvas awning frayed in many places. Steve halted to gaze, over a jumble of roof-tops, at a magnificent view of the far-distant harbour. Olive was seated at the farthest end of the balcony, in a deckchair, one foot supported by the wrought-iron railing, while she read a copy of *The Times* many days old. Briefly she lowered the newspaper to greet them, then raised it again. The three dogs began to approach her and then thought better of it, turning back into the room. As the largest passed Steve, it halted and gave a brief growl, as though unable to decide whether to nip him or not, before trotting on.

'I'll get two more cups,' Tilda said. The coffee was in an old-fashioned Cona machine, consisting of two glass globes, one above the other, with a spirit stove beneath them.

'Where is Guido?' Stefano asked.

'Sick.'

'Sick? He seemed perfectly well yesterday evening.'

Tilda shrugged. 'He says he has palpitations. *Chi lo sa?*'

'Palpitations? Well, that's not surprising when a heart is so old.'

Olive again lowered the newspaper. 'You must get rid of him. Retire him.'

'Easier said than done.'

Tilda had by now disappeared.

'The problem with you, Stefano, is that you're too soft-hearted.'

'How can I not be soft-hearted with Guido? He was with the family long before I was born. He gave so much time and so much care to looking after my father when he was dying.'

'That was only his job,' Olive said dismissively.

'How many people do a job with so much devotion?'

Olive turned to Steve. 'This man is *too* kind. Have you realised that?'

'Can one be too kind?' Steve asked with a laugh.

'Of course! People talk of being cruel only to be kind. But it's also possible to be kind only to be cruel. I know that Guido doesn't wish to quit, but to keep him on is a cruel sort of kindness.' She turned back to Stefano. 'What happened to you? One of Tilda's patients cancelled and so she prepared a delicious *piccata di vitello*. We waited and waited. I'd mixed the salad and all the leaves began to go limp and brown.'

'I'm sorry. I thought that she understood that we would be lunching out.'

'How can she understand something you fail to tell her?' Again she raised the newspaper.

Having handed the two men their cups of coffee, Tilda asked: 'So where did you eat then?'

'At the Palumbo d'Oro,' Stefano replied.

'Expensive.'

'Yes. Expensive. And today not very good. And crowded with people, most of them tourists.' He pondered for a moment, stroking his cheek with a hand. 'We had a rather unwelcome intrusion.' At that he switched to Italian.

At the end of his account, Olive exclaimed in English: 'That dreadful man! He's the laughing-stock of Palermo,' she added.

'Why do you have anything to do with him?' Tilda asked. 'The trouble is that you hate to be disagreeable. You must learn how to make enemies – as I learned a long, long time ago.' She put a hand to the braid of thick blonde hair which circled her head like a coronet and smiled more to herself than to the others in evident self-congratulation.

'I think that the problem is really a rather different

one.' Olive looked around her, as though she were about to make a wholly original pronouncement and wished no one present to miss it.

'How different?' Stefano asked.

'Well, part of you recoils from that kind of louche behaviour and part of you . . . is fascinated.'

'*Fascinated!*' Stefano's face began to redden. 'Fascinated! I am not in the least fascinated by Rudolfo as a man. All that fascinates me is his writing. Which is good. That's all, his writing. If I try to put up with him, it's for the sake of those plays. He is the best dramatist that Sicily has produced since Pirandello.'

Olive gave a loud, clear, derisive laugh. '*È cretino,*' she said.

Soon after that, Tilda began to interrogate Steve closely about his life. When she produced one particularly intrusive question – did he think that his mother and father had continued to have sexual intercourse after he, the younger of their two children, had been born? – Stefano intervened: 'You must forgive Tilda's probing. You must remember that she is a psychoanalyst.'

Increasingly embarrassed, Steve eventually put down his cup beside the Cona machine, and rose to his feet. 'I think I'll start on some exploring on my own, if you don't mind.'

'If you would like me to accompany you somewhere . . .' Stefano volunteered.

'No, no, thank you, thank you. You've already given me so much of your time.'

'You must do some more writing,' Tilda told Stefano. 'You know that.'

Stefano sighed. 'Yes, I know that. But so many other things seem so much more attractive.'

'You've always hated making any effort about anything,' Olive said. 'You have so many of the qualities necessary to write a novel – so much intelligence, sympathy, knowledge of the human heart. But . . . but . . . but. . .' She shrugged.

'Yes,' Stefano agreed abjectly. 'But . . . but . . . but . . . You are right, Olive *cara*, you are absolutely right.' Then he turned to Steve, who was standing awkwardly in the doorway leading from the balcony into the empty room behind him. 'Take the car if you wish.'

Steve shook his head. 'Thank you. I love walking. That's the best way to see a place.' Then he said: 'When I get back, I'll see if I can do anything about retuning that engine. But I'll have to find some better tools.'

'Oh, the garage can see to that. There's no need for you to bother. This is your holiday, your journey of a lifetime.' In the days ahead, Stefano, Tilda and Olive would often use that phrase 'the journey of a lifetime', bringing an affectionate mockery to it.

'No, no. I'd like to do it. As a small return – for all you have done for me . . .' Steve was thinking more at that moment of the majestic Bugatti than of the trivial little Fiat in the garage beside it.

Suddenly Olive pointed. 'You're wearing new shoes! And what beautiful ones!'

Now Tilda was also gazing at the shoes. 'Have you just bought them?' she asked. 'Those shoes can only be Italian.'

Before Steve, intensely embarrassed, could give any answer, Stefano said: 'I gave them to him as a present. Can you imagine – in this heat, constantly walking – he has nothing but a pair of heavy boots and some sandals? I had to buy him something comfortable and light.'

'They look as if they came from Ferrucci,' Olive said, staring once again at the shoes.

'Yes, they did.'

'It's a long time since I bought any shoes from Ferrucci,' Tilda said. She stretched out a leg and peered down at the flat-heeled brogue on her right foot.

'But *cara* – you have so many pairs of shoes. Many, many. And some of them you have hardly worn at all.'

Steve shifted from one foot to another and said: 'Well . . . I'll . . .'

He turned and began to pass into the empty room.

'*Ciao!*' Stefano called after him. 'See you soon, Steve!'

The two women were silent.

IV

Steve knocked on the door of Stefano's study and, when there was no answer, knocked again. Tilda, met in the cavernous hall as she was going out to a committee meeting of the animal protection society of which she and Olive were the most active, sometimes the only active, members, had said that the old man had been in there for hours. 'Perhaps he's fallen asleep. He often does. There's been no sound from him. Go in and wake him up. If he sleeps too long in the afternoon, he is bad-tempered for the rest of the day.'

Some time after the second knock – Steve was just about to knock yet again – a hoarse, tired voice called '*Avanti!*' Steve entered.

The fat, cigar-like cylinder of the malachite fountain pen in one hand and his other resting over the sheets of paper on the blotter, as though to defend them, Stefano squinted up. There was none of the usual warmth; he looked exasperated almost beyond endurance. 'Yes, what is it?' he snapped. His forefinger, Steve noticed, was stained with black ink. Like a melanoma, Steve suddenly thought, remembering the ominous, ever-growing black patch on his sister's arm.

'I'm afraid I'm disturbing you. I'm sorry.'

'What is it? *What – is – it?*' Stefano isolated each of the three words as he repeated them. 'Oh, come on!'

Steve stepped from the doorway into the room. He

stood before the desk, thinking that this was like an interview with the often harassed, always irritable headmaster of the overcrowded school which he had attended in Sydney. 'It's nothing important.'

'Let me be the judge of that. Oh, do hurry!' All at once Stefano was coughing. Between each cough, he gulped for air.

'I was looking again at the tools. In the garage this time. They're not much good, I'm afraid. Many of the things I need I just can't find. A lot are rusty.'

'Tools? Tools? What do you want tools for?'

Could he have forgotten? 'I was going to retune the Fiat engine for you.'

'Oh, leave that to Beppo at the garage round the corner. He can do it. You don't want to bother with that. I've told you that already. Enjoy yourself, see all you can.'

'But I'd *like* to do it. As I said before – it would be a small return. And after that, I might even have a try at getting the Bugatti on the road again.'

'But I don't *want* it on the road! Far too expensive!' Then Stefano relented. 'Perhaps tomorrow we can go over to see Beppo. We can talk it all over with him. He might let you work there. Of course I'd have to pay him something, Beppo never gives one anything for nothing, that's not his way. But never mind, never mind.'

Steve now backed towards the door. 'Well, I'd better leave you.'

Suddenly Stefano's face underwent one of its sudden transformations. No longer scowling, no longer with his eyes fixed in barely restrained fury on the face before him, he flashed one of his singularly sweet smiles. 'I think that you have brought me luck. Do you often bring people luck?'

Strangely other people, back in Australia, had also told Steve that he had brought them luck. Yet he had never thought of himself as a lucky person. 'How do you mean?'

'I was stuck. In my novel, I mean. I was so near the end, only ten, twenty pages, and I was stuck. Then I met you in the rain and brought you back to this house. And at once – hey presto! – I knew exactly how the book must finish, I could see clearly to the end of the road, every bend in it obvious to me! Most of last night I was working. And all this afternoon I have been working. Are you responsible for the miracle?' Steve stared at him, not answering. 'I think that perhaps you are. Perhaps you are the angel that troubled the waters.' He gave a wry, crooked little smile. 'The stagnant waters of my imagination.'

'Well . . .' Steve did not know what to answer. He shifted from one foot to another, staring down at the ground.

Stefano went on: 'I feared that it would be weeks, perhaps months, perhaps years, before the book was finished. But now – suddenly . . . *Un miracolo!* It will be only a few days – if my luck continues – the luck you brought me.' He raised both hands in the air and then let them fall, at the same time bursting into joyous laughter.

Steve found himself laughing too, he did not know why.

Then all at once Stefano pointed. 'You are wearing those terrible boots again.'

'I have to wear them for walking any distance. They're what I'm used to.'

'But they are terrible!'

'I'm sorry.'

'What's the use of my buying you an expensive pair of

shoes if you continue to wear those terrible boots?' Then, seeing the disconsolate expression on Steve's face, he relented. 'Oh, never mind! If you prefer your boots, then wear your boots! What does it matter?'

'Thank you.'

'Now you must leave me. No more interruptions! I have got to a very important paragraph, and I must get it written before dinner. I will see you at dinner, Steve. Eight thirty. But now . . .' He waved his hand in dismissal, as though he were shooing away a cat.

Beppo, who owned the garage, had a foxy, cheerful face, a scrawny body always tilted oddly to one side, as though his left leg were shorter than his right, and the feral smell, in no way disagreeable, of some penned animal. He spoke only a few words of English, learned in order to cope with the tourists who would from time to time appear for petrol or, far less frequently, to have their cars serviced. But despite the difficulties of communication, he and Steve got on well. He was in no way interested in the routine job of retuning the engine of the Fiat, but he shared Steve's enthusiasm for once more restoring the Bugatti to the road. '*Che bella!*' he had pronounced, narrow head tilted to one side under a clotted mop of grey-black hair and grease-soiled hands resting on filthy dungarees at his narrow hips, when, the work of the day over, he had accompanied Steve to the house to make an inspection. There and then he had suggested that he should fetch his pick-up truck and tow the car over to the garage.

Stefano, who was present, standing cautiously apart, had suggested that, since it was so late, Beppo might like to wait until the next day, but Beppo had insisted: no, no time like the present, his wife had gone to the cinema with her sister, he had nothing else to do until her return.

While the two men were working on the car, they would often become aware of a figure silently watching them from several feet away. Leaning on his gold-knobbed stick, Stefano would remain there for minutes on end. Then he would make a slow circle of the pit, now peering down at them and now peering into the interior of the Bugatti, as though he half expected its previous owner, his father, to be concealed somewhere inside it.

If Beppo were present, Stefano rarely said a word. But if Beppo were absent on some other job and Steve was therefore working by himself, then Stefano would talk to him. 'Why don't you leave that and see something more of Palermo?' he asked on one occasion. 'You can't spend your whole day working on a car. You have enough of that back home.' On another occasion, as Steve was straddling the engine, he cried out: 'Oh, those hands of yours! You're getting them filthy, you're chipping the nails. I hate to see that. It's as though – as though one of my Capodimonte figures were getting dirty and chipped.' Frequently he expressed admiration for the two men's dexterity – 'I couldn't learn to tighten a bolt as quickly and as efficiently as that in a thousand years,' or 'It's amazing how in a few seconds you get a truck so big into so small a space.'

Once, as he accompanied Steve back from the garage to the house, pausing from time to time to catch his breath even though Steve had slowed his usual rapid pace to his, he said: 'Steve, I must pay you for all this work. I must. It's not enough to pay Beppo. I must pay you.'

Steve shook his head. 'No. No, certainly not. You've been so kind to me, I'm living free. And anyway I *enjoy* the work. I really do.'

'But why should you *give* me your services – for so many days?'

'Have you forgotten what you once said about the pleasure of giving?'

'But still . . .'

Stefano made an impulsive gesture, putting out an arm as though he were about to throw it round Steve's shoulders. Then, as so often in the past, he just failed to do so. He drew a deep sigh. 'Oh, Steve, Steve. There's so much I want to say to you and somehow I can't.'

'Why not? Why not say it? Have I upset you in some way – done the wrong thing?'

'Oh, no, of course not! Of course not! Quite the contrary.'

'Well, then . . .'

Stefano shook his head. 'Another time perhaps. If I ever have the courage.' He sighed, turned his head away. 'My life has been full of unsaid things, full, full of them.'

'Oh, there's the library! Over there. I'd forgotten. They have some books for me. Perhaps you . . .? I don't feel like getting out of the car. Today I'm feeling rather *giù*. Would you mind, Steve? I'll stay here with Mimi.' Steve always hated it when Stefano brought along his favourite of the three Pekineses. She snuffled continuously and, though washed almost weekly by either Tilda or Olive, had a particularly unpleasant smell, at its worst when she stretched her mouth in one of her frequent yawns.

'Not at all. Provided someone understands what I'm

saying!'

'Park, park, park! Over there!' Suddenly imperious, as he could so often become, Stefano pointed. 'Hurry! That brute in that van will get in before you.'

'You don't mind waiting?'

'Of course not. I'd hardly have suggested your picking up the books for me, if I did. Now would I?' Then, the irritability vanishing as quickly as it had come, Stefano gave that sweet, hesitant smile of his. 'Sorry to put you to this trouble.'

As Steve opened his door, Mimi suddenly leapt off Stefano's lap, scampered over Steve's, and was out in the street. There was a screech of brakes as a van narrowly avoided hitting her.

'Oh, Steve! Steve! Get her! Get her!'

Steve raced after the bitch, which was now sniffing at a tattered bundle of greasy newspaper in the gutter, and eventually grabbed her. Snarling, she seemed about to bite his restraining hand.

'What gets into her?' Stefano asked, as Steve placed the dog once again on his lap. 'Usually she is so good and then a devil . . .' Suddenly he noticed the mingled exasperation and disgust on Steve's face. 'I have a feeling that you do not really like animals.'

'Oh, animals are all right by me. In fact, I do like them. But pets – it's pets that I'm not all that keen on.'

Stefano stared at him, clearly annoyed, his hand pulling at one of the dog's ears.

When, after endless delays, Steve at last emerged from the library weighed down by three volumes on nineteenth-century Sicilian history, he felt an immediate alarm. Stefano's body was slumped, awkwardly twisted round, against the window-side of the car, the back of his open right hand pressed against his mouth and the skin of his face giving off a strangely leaden luminescence. The dog was no longer in his lap but lay curled up on Steve's seat.

Steve opened the door on his side and peered in. 'Are you all right?'

'All right?' Stefano jerked up, he lowered his hand from his mouth. 'Of course I'm all right. Why? Why do you ask such a question?' His voice was hoarse and phlegmy. There were pearl-like beads of sweat on his forehead and on either side of his nose.

'I just thought . . . You looked . . .'

'I hate to be told how I look. Please never, never again tell me how I look.' Then, the irritability again vanishing, he gave a little laugh. 'Only the young and the beautiful should be told how they look.' He peered sideways at Steve, seemed about to say something further, then stopped himself. Eventually, as the car moved off, he asked: 'Any problems?'

'Not really. There was a girl there who spoke excellent English. But at first she couldn't find the books. That delayed me.'

'Typical!'

On arriving back at the house, Steve escorted Stefano into the hall, where he was told irritably: 'There's no need to come with me any further! Please! I can manage perfectly well.' After that, out of a sense of habit acquired over the years at the Sydney garage, Steve decided that he must brush the dust, blown through the open windows, out of the car.

It was then that, sniffing in distaste at Mimi's clinging

smell, he found the monogrammed handkerchief below Stefano's seat. It was stiff with dried blood.

Steve held it up by one corner and stared down at it.

For the first time, the piercing realisation came to him that Stefano must be seriously ill.

One evening at dinner Stefano told Tilda: 'You should see how that car looks now. Marvellous. All that rust seems to have disappeared. It looks just as it looked when, oh, years before the War, my father took it across the straits and we drove all the way to Geneva in it. Everyone admired it then. Everyone will admire it now.'

'I really cannot see the *point* of spending so much time on renovating a car which we're never going to use,' Tilda said. 'Olive was saying the same thing to me yesterday morning. What is the *point*? It'll eat up petrol. We'll never be able to afford it. Or are you planning to sell it once the work is finished?' She looked now at Steve and now at Stefano.

Stefano shook his head vigorously, setting down his knife and fork. 'Certainly not! I'd no more dream of selling it than of selling a family heirloom. That's what it is. A family heirloom.'

Tilda gave a scoffing laugh. 'A family heirloom! Are you crazy?'

'In its own way it's as beautiful as any heirloom in this house.'

'A car – beautiful!'

'Isn't it, Steve?'

Steve was embarrassed at being obliged to intervene in an argument between the two. 'Well, I don't know much about heirlooms,' he said. 'But to me it's, yes, beautiful.'

'Beautiful!' With a frown, Tilda picked up a piece of meat in her fingers, stooped, and offered it to the nearest of the dogs.

'Oh, no, no!' Stefano cried out. 'Not from the table!'

But, paying no heed, Tilda picked up another piece of meat and called: 'Mimi! Mimi! *Vieni!*'

From time to time, to be on his own, unnoticed, unhampered, uninvolved, Steve would make some excuse to absent himself from the house and the garage and would then wander aimlessly about Palermo. But the more he wandered, the more he hated the place. He had always been far happier in the country than in towns and cities, and his longing for the country now became acute. What was he doing here? Why didn't he move on? There was the old man, there was that car, a hugely magnified wasp, in the garage. Were those two things enough to hold him in thrall?

The streets were always crammed with people, their insistent identities battering at him. The streets were also always full of din – of vendors shouting their wares, of women screeching at each other from windows separated by the width of a busy thoroughfare, of cars hooting for no apparent reason, of Vespas roaring, their silencers removed, up side alleys and even on to pavements. No less offensive was the mess: of the carcasses of rusting cars, motor bicycles and bicycles, ravenously cannibalised and then left abandoned; of the scurf of bottles, newspapers and soiled wrappings piled high in the gutters and around every stunted tree; of dog and even human excrement in the park where, in an attempt to escape the ubiquitous squalor and noise, he once took himself.

One day, feeling thirsty, he had seated himself at a table outside a little café and ordered a Pepsi Cola. When he had paid, he had hesitated whether to leave a tip or not and then, remembering Stefano's example, had decided not to pocket the few coins which the waiter had reluctantly deposited in the saucer on which the bill had been presented. A wizened shoeshine boy had, at that moment, approached. He had pointed at Steve's scuffed boots: 'Shoeshine, mister?' Steve shook his head. Grinning, the boy said something in Italian. Again Steve shook his head. Again the boy said something in Italian. Then suddenly his small, grubby hand shot out, he scooped up the few coins and, with a yelp of triumph, raced off. Steve half rose, shouted 'Hey!' Then he gave up. It was too hot to run in pursuit. The loss was not his, but the waiter's. To his shock, he realised that all the people around him were either smiling or laughing.

On another occasion, Tilda had asked him to drive down to the market to buy some salad and fruit. It was a particularly oppressive day, the sky leaden and the air unusually humid. Steve stripped off his T-shirt and placed it on the seat beside him. At the market stall, he jumped out of the car, leaving the window open. On his return, only a minute or two later, with a lettuce, a bag of tomatoes and a hand of bananas, he realised that the T-shirt had vanished. He had seen no one approach the car, had heard not a sound. Had all the people around him similarly seen and heard nothing? Absorbed in their own concerns, they were not letting on.

Later, he told Olive of the two incidents when she asked him whether he liked Palermo. 'I suppose one just has to accept that one's living in a Third World country,' he concluded.

'A Third World country! What are you saying? You'd better not let any Italian hear you say that! Oh, do be careful! You'll get yourself beaten up or knifed!'

Was she being serious? He could not be sure.

V

At breakfast, Tilda asked Stefano: 'Is it tomorrow that you have to have your tests?'

Stefano nodded. 'The professor has returned from that conference in Detroit. Yes, he wants to see me tomorrow.'

In weary exasperation, Tilda put a hand to her forehead. 'Why didn't you remind me? I can't go with you tomorrow. You should have reminded me. I have this meeting – with that Englishman from the Royal Society for the Prevention of Cruelty to Animals. Don't you remember? He telephoned yesterday and without thinking I told him . . . He's coming on here from Naples as part of his tour. I can't put him off. Oh, why didn't you remind me when I was talking to him?'

Stefano laughed. 'Because, when you're talking to people on the telephone, you're always telling me not to listen.'

'Didn't the professor say that someone must bring you home when he had finished with you?' Tilda pursued. Stefano shrugged. 'I'm sure he did. He said that he was going to give you some kind of anaesthetic – or was it a tranquilliser? I can't ask Olive to go with you. She must meet this Englishman with me.' Chin cupped in palm, she stared morosely ahead of her. Then she said: 'Perhaps Louisa will be free . . . Or I might ask Renata.'

'Oh, not Louisa, not Renata! You know what I feel about both of them. No, I'll be perfectly all right. I can rest at the clinic until I feel well enough to come home.'

A half-eaten croissant held in a hand now deeply ingrained with oil, Steve leaned across the table. 'If you like, I could go with you.'

'*You?*' Tilda stared at him, as though he had made some totally outrageous suggestion.

Steve nodded. 'I could drive the Prince there in the Fiat and then I could wait for him. Easy. Why not?'

'Oh, Steve . . . Steve . . .' Stefano tilted his chair back, hands on the table as he smiled across it. 'Would you really? But that would interfere with your work on the car.'

'Only for a short while. What does that matter?'

'Oh, Steve . . . How wonderful of you! How kind you are!'

Steve felt embarrassed by a gratitude so much more intense than such a trivial offer could possibly deserve.

'I feel that the news is not good.' Stefano grimaced as, gazing up at the shiny white ceiling of the bare little room, he shifted uneasily on the narrow truckle-bed which, apart from a chair and rickety wooden table, comprised all the furniture.

'Why should you feel that?' But Steve himself also felt it, he could not have said why.

'That young woman doctor . . . There was something about the way in which, when I first went in, she was so talkative and friendly, and then all at once . . . There was something ominous – yes, really *ominous* – about the way in which she suddenly refused to meet my eyes and had virtually nothing to say . . .'

'I'm sure you imagined it.'

'Oh, Steve, Steve, Steve . . .' Stefano extended a hand, almost as though he expected Steve to take it, and then withdrew it quickly. 'It's so funny. For years I've not wanted to live, not much. And now I do, I do! Partly of course it's the book – so nearly finished, only a few pages more, after so many years. But that's not all. All at once, life . . .' Inertly, the hand which he had previously extended to Steve now toppled over the side of the bed. He shut his eyes. 'If only I could . . . If only . . .' He drew a deep sigh.

'You'd better sleep. There's no hurry to go home.'

'But you want to get back to that car. I'm spoiling your day.'

Steve shook his head, once more overcome by that tenderness which both surprised him and filled him with unease. It was as though, barely noticed, some alien wraith had slithered into him, to acquire more and more solidity and vigour and eventually to take him over. 'There's no hurry,' he said.

'But you have to get on with your journey of a lifetime.' As always, there was an affectionate mockery in Stefano's use of the phrase. 'I'm delaying you.'

'There's no hurry. The journey of a lifetime can wait.'

Once again, Steve felt that unaccustomed and therefore alarming tenderness surge up within him.

That night Steve had the Needle Dream.

. . . Once again a small boy of six or seven, barefoot, in his pyjamas, he is imprisoned inside a shiny drum like one of those in which his father stores his home-brewed wine. The drum is loaded on to his father's ramshackle truck, which is travelling at speed in a direction terrifyingly unknown to the boy. The drum is rolling from side to side, so that the boy, now forced to put his weight on one leg and now tilting over so that he is forced to put his weight on the other, has extreme difficulty in retaining his perilous balance.

Then, blinding in its brightness, the huge needle all at once appears. It is the size of a javelin, and its eye is like a giant, inflamed human one, red and raw, weeping a gluey substance. The needle begins to hurtle haphazard round the drum, just as on a summer night the forked lightning hurtles haphazard round the Sydney sky, while the child, looking wildly around him and leaping from side to side, struggles in panic to avoid it. At any moment, now, now, it will transfix him with its murderously sharp point. And all the time the terrified child is increasingly aware of a potent, nauseous smell. It is the smell that he always so much hates when he passes under the straggly, dusty pepper trees flanking the gate, rickety and askew, at the start of the uneven drive up to the house. It is a smell which he somehow associates with and yet does not want to associate with . . .

Steve let out a cry, thrashed from side to side, at last managed to jerk himself out of the nightmare as out of a quicksand closing above his head. Oh, Christ, Christ, Christ! Why should he have had that dream now, now of all times, after weeks of never having had it?

Well, at least here, so far from the main house, no one could have heard him cry out, as, embarrassingly, had happened in the Paris youth hostel.

VI

Tilda, in a towering fur hat like a guardsman's bearskin and a black coat buttoned up to her chin and reaching almost to her ankles, realised, as she was getting into the car, that she would have to take off the hat if it were not to scrape the roof. Settling herself with a sigh, she placed it on her lap. Steve, in his usual T-shirt and jeans, always wondered at her total imperviousness to the heat. What did she wear in the winter?

'You are kind to drive me,' she said. 'I hate driving at night, and Olive is not available.'

'It's nothing. What else have I to do? Beppo has gone home and locked up the garage.'

'Why do you waste your time on that car?'

'Because – oh – because I love it. In the same way as the Prince loves the old family palaces and all those pieces of furniture and pictures and . . . what he means by heirlooms.' He smiled. 'You know, I'd never heard that word before. I'd no idea what it meant. Perhaps some people in Australia have heirlooms. But my family don't. And none of the people I've met have ever had any.'

'Perhaps people like you are fortunate.'

'Fortunate?'

'Not to be encumbered by the past.' Suddenly, at that mention of the past, unbidden, there flashed back to Steve a memory of the fearful Needle Dream. It was like a shooting pain, a *tic douloureux*, momentarily agonising, then gone. 'That's really been my husband's trouble. All his life his ship has been in danger of sinking from all the things loaded on to it from the past. That's what has really prevented him from becoming a writer, instead of just wanting to become a writer.'

'But he's writing now.'

Tilda frowned and bit on her full lower lip. 'Yes.' She stroked the hat with the palm of the hand not holding it. 'That is what is so strange. Suddenly he is writing. He is old, tired, ill. But at last he is writing. Incredible! Why? Why?'

'Will the novel make him famous?'

Tilda shrugged. 'I have no idea. I haven't read it.'

'You haven't read it?'

Tilda laughed. Then she again stroked the fur of the hat, as though she were stroking one of her dogs, deliberately, tenderly. 'I haven't read it. He never lets anyone read anything he has written until it is finished. Yet I discuss my cases with him before they are finished. He even looks at the case-notes.' There was a silence. Then she said in a strangely listless voice: 'You know that he's a very sick man?'

'I guessed that.' He all but told her of his discovery of the blood-stiff handkerchief. 'It's serious?'

She nodded. 'The professor did not like the result of that bronchoscopy. Now he wants to perform an exploratory operation. But Stefano doesn't want to go into the clinic until the book is finished.'

'That won't be long, will it?'

'With him you can't be sure how long anything will take.'

'What exactly is the matter with him?'

'The professor thinks it may be something – serious.'
She turned her head to him. 'Although I have a medical
training, there is one disease I have a superstitious terror
of naming. You can guess what it is.'

Steve nodded. He could guess. 'But that's – terrible . . .'
Suddenly, although he had known Stefano for so short a
space of time, he was overwhelmed with sadness.

Tilda shrugged. 'It *may* be terrible. But until he has that
exploratory operation we cannot be sure.'

The drive continued in silence until, near the centre of
the town, Tilda said: 'Oh, I've just remembered. Could
you please stop here for a moment? Yes, by this
restaurant. I want to tell my girl-friend Louisa something.
She is having dinner here. The birthday party of someone
I do not know.'

Tilda had many 'girl-friends', Steve had noticed, most
of them middle-aged women, who dressed quietly but
expensively, who often had uniformed chauffeurs to wait
outside the house for them when they called, who were
rarely accompanied by their men-folk, although most of
them were married, and who had a way of lowering their
voices to all but a whisper when talking to Tilda in his
presence, even though they knew that he could not speak
Italian.

Clutching the long coat around her, as though against
an icy wind, Tilda swept in. Steve reached for the
crumpled Italian newspaper abandoned by Stefano in the
car that morning, and stared at its front page. There was
a picture of Andreotti, who had once again been elected
Prime Minister; but Steve did not know who Andreotti
was. Then he opened the paper and looked at another
picture, of Anna Magnani. He did not know who she was

either.

It was at that moment that, through the doors of the restaurant, thrown wide open because of the heat, he heard the violinist. He was playing 'Santa Lucia' with a gypsy's exaggerated portamento, lingering now on one note, like a bee sucking all the sweetness out of a flower, and then gliding with a drunken voluptuousness to another, where he repeated the process. Steve could see him now: a squat, dark-faced man – yes, he might indeed be a gypsy – in tight black trousers with gold braid down their sides, and a sleeveless jacket glittering under the light with gold braid and gold buttons. He was at a long table crowded with people, at least twenty – perhaps this was the birthday party attended by Tilda's 'girl-friend'? – but no one paid any attention to him, chattering and laughing and eating and drinking, while he bent over now one woman and now another and the bow soughed and sighed its sentimental twaddle. One of the men, his silver hair and his gold pince-nez glittering under the light beneath which he was seated, drew out his wallet and removed a note, which he then furtively tucked into a pocket of the violinist's waistcoat.

It was when the violinist moved on to another table, where a young girl and an old man faced each other, that suddenly Steve felt that he could stand the music not a moment longer. Like his father, he was one of those rare people who have perfect pitch, and he could sing, if obliged to, in a light, easy tenor. But he hated music, and violin music most of all. It perturbed him, it could even fill him with panic, as it was doing now.

. . . A boy of seven, with skinny, bare legs and huge eyes of an arctic blue, is reading a comic in the small, untidy sitting-room, while elsewhere two people are crying. One of them, whose crying erupts in desperate, gulping wails, is his thirteen-year-old sister in the narrow room, once a box-room, which became hers when their father decided that she was now too old to sleep in the same room as her brother.

The other person crying is the boy's mother, in the kitchen where, in slippers and a wrap-around cotton dressing-gown, her hair in curlers, she is standing over a sink and washing up the things from the tea (for them, as for their neighbours, that meal is always tea) which has just ended in such a hurricane of emotion. She is crying softly, so softly that she imagines that no one can hear her. Above all, she does not wish her husband to hear her, since she wishes him to think that she is totally impervious to anything that he may do to her. That imperviousness is the only revenge that she can get on him.

The girl upstairs is still in the torn dress which has been the cause of the hurricane. It once belonged to her mother, who then painstakingly, over many days, made it over for her, so that she could attend a birthday party given by the boy-friend whom eventually she will marry not so much out of love for him as out of hatred for her home. The girl begged the mother not to make the dress look *square*, and so, at her urging, the mother cut it daringly low at front and back and daringly short, so that it revealed not merely the girl's dimpled knees but also an expanse of her plump thighs.

When she came down late to the tea spread out on the kitchen table, the father jumped up and yelled: 'Christ! You're not going to wear that!' When he was enraged as now, his Lithuanian accent became much thicker.

Without saying anything, eyes downcast, the girl took her place and reached across first for a piece of bread and then for a slice of ham.

'What the fuck are you wearing?' He had begun to drink from a bottle of his home-made 'Dubonnet' as soon as he had got home from work. At work, repairing and decorating the houses of others, as he never has time to repair and decorate the house which he now at last, the mortgage paid off, can say is truly his, he had all through the day swigged from cans of lukewarm beer.

Still the girl, eyes downcast, said nothing. She bit into the slice of bread, held so daintily in a small hand the nails of which her father has forbidden her ever to paint; and then she put that down and picked up her knife and fork and cut into an overripe tomato, its juice squirting out like blood over the plate and spattering the flowered plastic cloth.

He turned to the mother. 'Did you make that dress like that? Is that your doing?'

Impassively, gazing out of the window, the mother sipped her tea.

'You're not going out wearing that! Not on your fucking life!'

The girl rose, the slice of half-eaten bread, a trace of lipstick where her teeth had bitten into it, still in her hand. She said coldly: 'I'll wear what I like!'

'Oh, no, you fucking won't!'

The mother went on eating her tea. She did not look at either her husband or her daughter. Her face, with its high Slavic cheekbones and its deep-set eyes, of the same strangely pale blue as her son's, showed no emotion, except that there was now about it a white, clammy chill. Soon she will take a lover, one of her husband's closest friends, 'a confirmed bachelor' (that is how people have always described him), also a Lithuanian, who works with her husband and who for many years has lived in a boarding-house up the road. Soon she will quit the house, taking a job as a waitress at a local café. The boy now stared at her, willing her to do something, though he knew that she never would, since she had never done so in the past, when the father had thrashed him or his sister, locked them up for hours on end in their room, or refused them food as a punishment for some trivial misdemeanour or for what he calls (having learned the phrase from the people with whom he has worked) 'bloody lip'.

'We'll see about that.' The girl was defiant.

Suddenly, with an inarticulate bellow, the father leapt from his chair. The chair toppled backwards and crashed to the floor. He gripped the girl by one arm and then, as she turned her face, contorted with pain, away from him, he dragged her round until his snarling lips all but touched her trembling ones. 'Listen to me, madam!' He pronounced that last word as though it were the French *madame*. 'You just bloody listen to me. I'm not having no daughter of mine going out looking like a prostitute. It's just not on. Get it?'

She wrenched herself free.

'If you want to go to that fucking party, you just put on something more respectable.'

'Leave me alone! I'll wear what I want! You can't dictate to me!'

Again he emitted that inarticulate bellow of rage. It

reminded the terrified little boy of the distant baying he sometimes heard emerging from the zoo which he had often wanted to visit but, for lack of the entrance money, had never done so. Then the father grabbed at the dress where the skirt was taut over the girl's plump thighs. 'Take this off! Take it bloody off!'

She jerked away. He clutched tighter at the skirt. There was a ripping sound. The girl screamed: 'Now look what you've done! Now look!' She stared down, aghast, at the jagged rent in the gauzy material. Then she let out the first of those gulping wails as she raced up the stairs.

Later her boy-friend will arrive to fetch her to his party, and the mother will tell him, in a calm, seemingly unconcerned voice, that her daughter has been taken sick, no, nothing serious, just one of those women's things. Out of a mingling of loyalty and shame, the girl has never spoken to the boy of what goes on in her home. But the neighbours gossip about the 'foreigners' at the farthest end of the road – about the way in which they keep themselves to themselves, about the bruises and abrasions which can so often be seen on the children, about the way in which on a Sunday the father forages for wild mushrooms on the hills, about the mother's frugality in buying from the local store, now run by a couple from Salonica, food long past its sell-by date and so drastically reduced in price.

Now alone in the sitting-room, lying on his stomach on the floor in a corner, the boy turns over the pages of the comic. But he is taking nothing in. He is listening to those two women sobbing. Then suddenly he is aware that his father is standing at the foot of the stairs. Like his son's in adulthood, his is a firm, muscular, sunburned body; but

unlike his son's, this body is matted with hair. The boy
hates that pelt-like hair, the mere sight of it nauseates
him. More than once he has referred to his father as 'the
gorilla' when talking of him to his sister. He can see a lot
of the hair because, in the heat and humidity of that late
summer evening – Christmas is already past – his father
has now stripped down merely to a pair of baggy, creased
boxer shorts. His feet, with their curved, hornlike nails,
are bare and white, and out of the pelt on his chest the
unusually prominent nipples gleam pink. He is holding
his violin, bought many years ago off the widow of a man
who played in the Sydney Symphony Orchestra, in one of
those surprisingly beautiful, long-fingered hands (his son
has inherited them) and the bow in the other. He places
the violin under his chin, he raises the bow. The son puts
his hands over his ears, even though the last time that he
did that his father kicked him not once but a number of
times with a demented ferocity.

His father begins to play, a dreamy expression in those
eyes which so recently were blazing. He plays a waltz –
Strauss, Waldteufel, Lehar? – and as he does so, indulging
in the same exaggerated portamento as the violinist in
the restaurant, he closes his eyes and sways in time to the
music. He looks suddenly contented, even happy. It is
only when he plays the violin and after he has had an
orgasm with the wife who merely suffers his brutal
thrusting, having no part in it, that he looks like that.

The boy keeps his hands over his ears, removing the
right one only to turn over the pages of the comic of
which he is taking in nothing.

. . . At last Tilda emerged from the restaurant in her
towering shako. 'Sorry about that.' Then: 'Are you all

right?' She had noticed something odd about Steve's face: the muscles of the jaw unusually taut, the colour bled away under the tan, the eyes almost desperate.

'Oh, yes, I'm fine, fine.' He turned the key in the ignition. He wanted only to get away from the mendacious swooping and swooning of that violin held close to the ears of the embarrassed, unwilling customers in the overcrowded, noisy restaurant.

VII

The next day Steve drove the Fiat down to Stefano's club to fetch him home after he had been attending a luncheon held there by a literary circle to which he belonged. 'It's called "Il Circolo di Martedì", because many, many years ago, when I was still a schoolboy, it met every Tuesday,' Stefano told Steve. 'Now it meets on the second Monday of every month. But the name has not changed. That's Sicily for you.'

Although Stefano had drawn a neat little map on a sheet of thick, cream-coloured vellum heavily embossed with the family crest, Steve managed to lose his way and so arrived more than twenty minutes late. In consequence, although Stefano had said that he would be waiting in the entrance at three thirty, there was now no sign of him.

An elderly porter in a shabby, creased dark blue uniform, stained with sweat under the arms and at the collar, stared haughtily at Steve and then demanded: '*Sì, signore?*'

Steve explained in English that he had come for Stefano and then endured a contemptuous scrutiny, similar to Guido's, as the porter's gaze took in his T-shirt, jeans and scuffed boots. Eventually the porter said something in Italian and, when Steve frowned in incomprehension, waved a hand in the direction of a door further up the reception area with a barked: '*Là!*

Colá!

Stefano, knees drawn up and a hand under a cheek, looked extraordinarily small and vulnerable, an aged, ailing, tired child, as he slept nestled up in a vast leather armchair. His mouth was open and a thread of saliva glittered on his chin. His cheeks were unnaturally flushed.

Reluctant to wake him, as years later he would be reluctant to wake his sleeping children even though a failure to do so would make them late for school, Steve stared down at the old man. Then he ventured, in almost a whisper: *'Principe! Principe!'* So often Stefano had told him to call him by his Christian name, but somehow he had never been able to do so. Louder, he repeated: *'Principe!'*

Stefano stirred, emitted a little chirrup. Then his eyes opened, startled. For several seconds he stared up at Steve, as though he had never seen him before and had no idea who he might be.

'I'm late, I'm afraid.'

'Steve! Oh, Steve!' Suddenly his face was irradiated not merely with pleasure but with joy. 'Steve! Wonderful!'

His feet went down to the worn carpet. He began to struggle to rise. Steve put out a hand and the old man gripped first it and then the arm above it. The grip was surprisingly firm. He had never before touched Steve. Steve gave him a heave and he smiled in gratitude and said: 'How strong you are!'

Once in the car, he said: 'That was such a boring occasion. Why do I go on attending those meetings? All those people talking about nothing but themselves – their silly little books, their silly little lives, their silly little ideas of how to make Sicily prosperous and well governed. I'd have much rather had luncheon with you. Did you eat alone or did Tilda join you?'

'The Princess joined me. And two of her friends.'

'Two of her "girl-friends"?' He asked it sardonically.

Steve nodded. 'I can't remember their names. I've never met them before.'

'I usually can't remember their names either.'

At Stefano's direction, Steve now turned into a wide street unfamiliar to him. He saw a long, red-brick building, with people hurrying up and down its cracked marble steps. 'Is that the main post office?'

'That's right. Haven't you seen it before?'

'Sometime I ought to go there.'

'Why? You can buy stamps at that little shop in the street behind us.'

'I told people to write to me there poste restante. To the main post office.'

'And you've been here so many days now and you've never been there to collect your letters?' Stefano was incredulous.

'Probably there aren't any.'

'But don't you want to know what has been happening to your family and friends?'

Steve could not answer. He wanted to know and yet he shrank from knowing, since he felt that that knowledge might imperil his new-won sense of freedom – just as any attachment to Stefano or anyone else met on his travels might also imperil it.

'I might come back here later this afternoon.'

'No, no! Let's go in now!'

Steve was reluctant but Stefano prevailed upon him.

'You can park there, there! In the forecourt of that shop. They know me there, that's where I go for my shirts. They won't mind If we use some of their space.'

'I'll only be a moment.'

'I'll come with you.'

Having seemed to have been on the verge of death when Steve had approached him in the club drawing-room, Stefano was now full of energy. He scrambled out of the car, reached for his panama hat and cane from the back seat, and then preceded Steve up the marble steps at a brisk pace.

Steve hated to have other people do things for him. He wished that Stefano would let him ask for the letters, however difficult that might be with no Italian, instead of himself assuming that task. Impatiently, almost angrily, he listened as Stefano spelled out his name in Italian. They then waited as the clerk retreated into a long corridor behind his booth and began to edge slowly down the rows of pigeon-holes, many of them crammed with letters which had the appearance, murky and musty, of having languished there for many years.

Eventually the clerk returned with a single airmail letter. He held it out. '*Eccovi!*'

'Is that all?'

Stefano repeated Steve's question in Italian.

The clerk nodded and raised his shoulders and arms in an extravagant gesture which said: 'Yes, that's all. But why that's all, don't ask me!'

However, at Stefano's urging, the clerk eventually again went back, with a noisy sigh, into the corridor of pigeon-holes and renewed his search. It was with evident satisfaction that he then announced: '*Niente di piú, principe. Mi dispiace.*'

Stefano looked searchingly into Steve's chagrined face. 'You are disappointed,' he said.

'No, not really.'

'Yes, you are disappointed. Only one letter. Poor Steve! But, you know, in Italy letters constantly get lost. Or delayed. Possibly many people have written to you and the letters have gone to the wrong city or are somewhere here in the wrong place. Yes, yes! It's possible, perfectly possible.'

Steve said nothing.

Back in the car, Steve propped the letter on the dashboard and then turned the key in the ignition.

'Don't you want to open your letter?'

'Oh, not now. I can read it when we get home.'

'But it might have something important in it.'

Steve smiled. 'It's from my mother.'

'Well, then . . . Isn't that all the more reason . . .?'

'Nothing important ever happens to her.' He had been disappointed that there had been no letter from his former lover Sue. Throughout the journey he had often thought of her and dreamed of her, and had willed her to write to him. All his life he had believed that, if he willed something with sufficient concentration and force, he could achieve it.

'Aren't you fond of your mother?'

'Yes, very much.'

'What a strange boy you are!' Although Steve was twenty-four it was always as a 'boy' that Stefano spoke of him.

'Am I? Stranger than other people?'

'Well, not stranger than *me!*'

Even when he was once more back in his own room, Steve

did not immediately open his mother's letter. He removed his boots, T-shirt and jeans and then, in only his underpants, went into the bathroom, where he spent a long time splashing cold water over his face, arms and chest. Each time that the ice of the water met the heat of his skin, he gave a gasp of mingled shock and pleasure.

After he had dried himself, he still left the letter on the bed, where he had first thrown it. Standing at the open window, he gazed down into the courtyard. He could hear the irregular lisping of the fountain – sometime, as soon as he had finished with the Bugatti, he would rid the marble basin of its weeds and unblock those of its faucets which no longer functioned – and, far off, he could also hear the distant roar of the traffic. Suddenly he felt a longing to get out of this city into the countryside which, from his early childhood, had always had the power to console, calm and heal him when his spirits or even his body were lacerated and bruised.

When his father had been on the rampage (that phrase was his mother's), Steve would often slip out of the house and make his way first along an unmade road and then along a path which led up, through thick undergrowth, into the hills. He rarely met anyone and, if he did, he never exchanged a glance, much less said a word. He had certain secret places - secret even from his sister – where he would sit, scrutinising the life, so different from his own, of the birds and the small animals around him. Sometimes he would pick wild flowers for his mother, who would then arrange them in a milk-bottle or a jam-jar, where they would soon droop and wither.

Later in his life, when he had quit his home and had moved on from his sister's house to a small rented room in the heart of Sydney, he would spend each weekend tramping the countryside, all alone, with a backpack. He would bed down on bracken or a pile of leaves, wash in a stream or pool, not bother, even in winter, about hot food or drink. Often he hated the work of the garage, with its endless relay of music from a loudspeaker, its clamorous voices, its clanging of metal on metal, its constant toing and froing. He would not have been able to bear that life but for his weekend escapes. His colleagues, who both liked him and were puzzled by him, would from time to time suggest a weekend jaunt or party. To evade such invitations, he eventually invented a girl-friend, living on a farm far away from the city, whom he regularly visited. They would tease him about this girl-friend. He did not care.

Slowly he moved back from the window and approached the bed. He took up the envelope, which had become heavily creased, almost as though someone, his mother or a post office worker, had folded it in four, and examined his name on it. Then he turned it over and, frowning now, examined his mother's name and her address, both written in her bold, childish writing. Amazingly, some five years before, she had won two hundred thousand Australian dollars in a lottery. This had enabled her to buy herself a bungalow in a pleasant suburb of Sydney and to advance him the money which he had needed before he could secure a mortgage on a run-down house which, totally rehabilitated, he had first let out and then sold at a profit to finance this 'journey of a lifetime'.

He inserted a forefinger into the flap of the envelope. It proved oddly unyielding, just as his mother herself had always proved oddly unyielding when he had attempted to penetrate her life before her arrival in Australia and her marriage to his father. Her mother, a sister and a brother had all perished in a concentration camp – where, he never discovered – which, by some miracle or freak, she had somehow survived. But when he tried to question her further about all these horrors, she would merely say: 'Sorry, Steve. I don't like to talk about it. The past is the past.'

What she did not mind talking about was her arrival, in her teens, as a refugee in Australia, her years in a convent (it must have been then that she was converted from her ancestral faith to Roman Catholicism), and her subsequent work as a bus conductor. It was while at work on a bus that she had met, at one and the same time, the man who was to become her husband and the man who was to become her lover. Both were then employed as labourers in the harbour, and both travelled each day to their work on her bus. 'Your father literally fell for me,' she would often recount. Exhausted, she had been sitting on the long seat by the entrance to the bus. When it had jerked over a pot-hole, one of the two men, having just entered, was thrown into her lap. If it had been the man who became her lover, instead of the man who became her husband, her whole life would certainly have been different and might even have been better, she would speculate – 'But then I'd never have had you and your sister.'

Steve began to read. Although his mother's hand was so clear, his eyes travelled slowly from one letter to another. His lips moved and then moved again as, correcting a misreading, he repeated some word over to himself yet again. Her solipsism had always exasperated him and it exasperated him now. His own letters to her, so laboriously inscribed and so full of mistakes of spelling and grammar, were in the nature of a diary, recording all the places which he had visited and all the people whom he had met. But beyond writing 'It was lovely to get those six letters of yours, what a surprise to have two arrive, one from Vienna and one from Prague, on the same day!', she made no further reference to them. Everything else was about her own narrow little life in her narrow little suburb: about the hen which, mysteriously, had stopped laying, though seemingly healthy; about the pair of shoes which had proved such a bad buy, letting in the rain; about the new neighbour, a young widow, who was always so helpful in providing lifts into town; about the faulty lavatory flush – if only Steve were there to see to it for her . . .

Eventually, he threw the letter down on to the bed beside him, its third page unread. Sometime, later that day or tomorrow or the day after, he would take it up again and persevere with it to its end. Still seated on the bed, he put his elbows on his bare knees and propped his head on his palms. At long last he allowed himself to savour the full bitterness of the fact that the letter for which he had been hoping ever since he had looked in vain for it first in Paris and then in Rome, had yet again failed to arrive. Was it because he had really known all along that it would fail to arrive, that he had delayed, to Stefano's obvious amazement, any visit to the post office? Yes, that could be it, that could be it.

. . . Sue and he had eventually come to make love not in his flat, as at the beginning of their relationship, but in

hers. His flat, she said, was so far out and she did not like
to waste the time which it took to get to it, now that the
programme kept her so busy. But what she really meant
was that her own flat, in a modern block with a porter, was
so much more attractive than his, in a dilapidated thirties
house built in so gimcrack a fashion that one could
constantly hear the Greek tenants above – shouting at
each other or playing their relentless bouzouki music or
making love or merely stomping about.

Hers was one of the most popular children's
programmes ever to have gone out on Australian
television, and she herself had become so popular in it
that, as she and Steve walked through the streets, people
would stare, point, smile, nudge each other, and even
hold out scraps of paper for a signature.

Sue and he had met long before her days of success.
Then, a drama student, she worked at night as a waitress
in a self-service café opposite his flat. Her widower father,
who was English, was a professor at the university, his
subject so obscure to Steve – palaeontology, plantology,
pathology? - that he could never remember what it was. In
turn the professor could never remember whether Steve's
father and mother had come from Lithuania or Estonia.
When he apologised for getting their provenance wrong,
he would always say: 'Well, I know it's somewhere up there
in the north and part of the Soviet Empire.' This well-to-
do man - he had a private income, inherited from an
aunt, in addition to his salary – did not believe in giving
his children what he called 'crutches'. That was why Sue
worked in the café while still a drama student.

Steve would go into the café and drink cup after cup of
coffee, even though, still saving to buy the house of which

he dreamed and in which he was never to live, he hated to waste the money. The coffee would then keep him awake, and he would toss from one side to another of the wide bed given to him by his mother when she and her lover had separated and she had no further use for it, and think of Sue. Guiltily he would often masturbate, since all too often that was the only way to quieten his trilling nerves.

Eventually he summoned the courage to ask Sue to go trekking with him over a weekend. They would travel on his motor bike, he told her, and he would show her the Blue Mountains. How about that? At the time she seemed enthusiastic. But once they had started on the journey, she was full of complaints. The dust was getting into her hair, which she had washed and set only that morning, it was also getting into her throat and making her hoarse. Later, she complained of the bed-and-breakfast establishment, at which she demanded a room to herself – the nylon sheets looked dirty, she had seen a cockroach in the bathroom, why did the bacon and eggs have to be so greasy? That was the last time that he took her into the country which he loved so much. 'Basically I'm a town girl,' she declared. Her town had been London. Sydney for her was an inferior sort of town, but even so it was infinitely better than the country.

Eventually they were lovers. In bed she was like a small child, giggling a lot and saying 'Let's just have a little snog, let's not get too intense,' and suddenly deciding that she had had enough of the love-making and wanted to do something else – to go to a late-night cinema or take a stroll or merely eat a bowl of cereal or some buttered toast in the kitchen. Perhaps it was this essential childishness which accounted as much for her success in the programme as did her comeliness and her air of well-being and health.

As that success increased, so she increasingly nagged at him to quit his job in the garage, to educate himself, to *get a move on*. In this she was seconded by her father. 'You're really very intelligent,' he would tell Steve in a languid voice belied by his university reputation of being a man who got things done with uncompromising ruthlessness. 'It's such a pity that you left school at sixteen and that you never really had a proper education before that. I wonder if it's now too late for you to do something about it?' Sue would then butt in to say that Steve was getting jolly well paid at the garage. In turn her father would correct her: 'We're not talking *money*, Sue dear. We're talking quality of life.'

Steve and Sue were in that flat of hers, lying side by side, having made not very satisfactory love – 'We must get on with it,' she had told him when, naked, he had clambered on to the bed beside her, 'I have that rehearsal at almost dawn tomorrow and must have an early bed' – and the fingers of one of his hands were gently tugging at one of her nipples. It was then, on an impulse, that he decided to tell her of his plans for the journey of a lifetime. He had found, he told her, a buyer for the house, a German in the wine trade, who was prepared to pay a sum way beyond his expectations. He would invest half the proceeds of the sale and the other half he would 'blue' (he used that word) on a year of freedom such as he had never known before.

He had expected Sue to protest 'But what about me?' and he had already prepared what he would answer –

couldn't she start out with him or join him at some point, or even take a whole year off herself? But instead she merely said: 'Oh, I think that's the most wonderful idea.'

It was he who then said: 'But what about us?', adding: 'That's the thing that worries me.'

She looked at him, coolly, appraisingly; and, chilled by that look, he released the swollen nipple, propped his body up on an elbow, and stared down at her, waiting apprehensively for long, long seconds for her answer. But none came.

Eventually he said: 'You think I should throw up the job at the garage and go?'

'Yes, of course! Jobs in garages aren't difficult to find. Not if one is a good mechanic. Which you obviously are.'

'But what about us?' he repeated.

'Us?' She swung her legs off the bed and reached for her wrap. She pulled the wrap around her and then sat on the edge of the bed in brief thought. Then, head on one side, so that her long, straight, reddish-blonde hair screened her face from him, she said: 'Don't you think that perhaps we're coming to the end of the road?'

'What do you mean?' When she did not answer with anything other than a sigh, he went on, with a simplicity which later was to touch her each time that she recalled it at some rare moment of discouragement or loneliness: 'Don't you love me any more?'

Again she sighed. Then she said: 'Oh, this is all so boring. Loving, not loving! I don't know, I just don't know. Oh, I'm *fond* of you. You have such a sweet, tender, sunny nature. Yes, of course I'm *fond* of you. But love . . . ' She got off the bed and fetched herself a cigarette from a packet on the dressing-table. He was constantly begging her not to smoke, even in those days when smoking had not yet become a social liability. He hated the smell of tobacco on her breath, in the kitchen, above all in the lavatory. She blew out smoke through the nostrils of her small, upturned nose. (It was that nose which had caused Steve's mother once to remark to him that Sue had 'a rather piggy look'. Steve had been furious.) Then she said: 'We're growing apart. I've had that feeling for some time.' He stared at her, uncomprehending and stricken. 'Our lives are diverging,' she amplified. 'All the time. You in that garage of yours. While I have . . .' She restrained herself from saying 'I have my increasingly successful career, my mounting income, my intellectual friends, my father who is a professor, my dream of returning to England and achieving television stardom there as well . . .'

'So you mean – this is the end?'

She laughed. 'Oh, not the *end!* But that was precisely what she did mean. Later she was to tell her father: 'The sad fact is that I've outgrown him' and he was to nod sagely: 'Well, he was never good enough for you.' 'Just a break,' she went on, 'a much-needed break, during which we can sort out ourselves and our relationship . . .'

. . . Steve jumped off the bed and once again went to the window. He stared out at the fountain, its erratic jets glittering in the sunshine of the late afternoon. He had written her many letters, consulting his pocket dictionary to check his spelling and pondering each word with care. But now he knew that he would never get a letter back from her.

Suddenly his face crumpled, as he put a hand up to it and over it. A moment later the arctic blue eyes were flooded with tears.

Still at the window, his hands now on his narrow hips, he eventually again began to think of his mother.

. . . It is late in the evening. The boy and the girl have been sent up to bed in the room, scrupulously tidy because that is how their father insists that it should be, which they both share. In a few months they will be physically separated, just as they will be emotionally separated by the girl's acquisition of a boy-friend, but now they are as close as Steve and a woman will ever be close.

Steve is the first to be roused by the shouting. He sits up in bed, his head supported on an elbow, and listens, his heart thudding more and more painfully, as though it were the only thing in his otherwise hollow body. The girl also sits up with a start. In silence, both strain to hear.

Then the girl creeps out of bed and, having opened the door with extreme care, tiptoes out on to the landing. The boy follows her. They stand so close to each other that their bodies are almost touching.

'You stupid cunt! *Answer me!* Answer me! What the fuck have you and he been getting up to? Answer!'

But the mother, who is ironing, does not answer.

The boy turns and looks into his sister's face. He is suddenly destroyed by the expression on it. He has never before seen that expression of dread, desolation, hopelessness. In the years ahead, when she has become a plump, seemingly happy, seemingly self-confident wife and mother, he will look at her and then, suddenly, he will have the illusion of seeing that expression yet again. It will be as though he had all at once been granted the cruel ability, totally unsought and totally unwanted, to Xray a palimpsest.

The father is still yelling his obscenities. 'What has he done to you? How often has he fucked you?'

Who is this 'he'? The boy has no idea.

Oh, why doesn't she answer him back? Rush out of the house? Pick up the iron and – yes, yes, yes! – slam it into his face?

The boy does not appreciate that this calm, cold silence of hers is a far more potent weapon than a heated iron or any angry, recriminatory words.

. . . Steve went back to the bed, picked up his mother's letter, and reluctantly forced himself to read on from where he had left off.

It was only then that he had realised, for the first time in his life, that his mother was the sole person who had ever got the better of his father.

VIII

At first, when she drove into the garage in the low-slung MG, its hood down, Steve did not recognise her. She was wearing huge dark glasses and a peaked white cap tipped jauntily over an eyebrow. '*Steve!*' she called. 'Steve!' It was Olive. 'Do come over here a moment!'

He got up from his crouching position beside the Bugatti – years later, because of that constant crouching, he was to have endless trouble with a disc – and, hand pressed to the small of his back, walked stiffly across to where, engine still coughing away, she had stopped the car. 'One of the front lights needs fixing,' she said. 'Do you think you could do that for me?'

'Oh, you'd better speak to Beppo about that. He'll get one of the men to do it.'

She pouted, at the same time pulling off the dark glasses to reveal popping eyes glistening with mascara. 'Oh, but I'm sure you'd do it much more quickly and efficiently.'

'I doubt it. His men are good. In any case, I'm not here working for him. I'm just working on that car for the Prince.' He pointed.

'Oh, well, never mind! It was just a thought. I'll talk to Beppo about it some other time. He seems to be busy with a customer.' In the office, Beppo, a half-eaten bar of chocolate in one hand, was chatting to a man in a charcoal grey suit and a grey fedora. Olive gave Steve a cheeky smile. Then she said: 'There was something else. I gather you fixed that ancient hoover for Guido. Yes?' Steve nodded. 'Mine – which is even more ancient – seems to have given up the ghost. I was wondering . . . Could you . . .?'

'Well, yes,' Steve agreed reluctantly. 'Of course. I could look in some time tomorrow – or perhaps even this afternoon. But I don't know if . . . I'm not an expert on hoovers, only on cars. In the case of the Princess's hoover it was just a matter of a faulty connection.'

'The thing is I – I wonder if you could come *now?*'

'*Now?*' Steve was getting near to the end of his work on the car. He had no wish to interrupt it. Already he was dreaming of quitting the city and making his way first into the interior of the island and then across the straits to Sardinia, and so on to – well, where, where? His ideas of geography were vague, but he knew that he must see Egypt, Turkey, Greece and then, on his long swing back home, Iran, India, Thailand, Malaysia, Indonesia . . .

'If that's possible. I'd pay you of course,' she added. 'That must be *bien entendu.*' Steve had no idea what she meant by that last phrase. 'You see, two of the bedrooms really must be hoovered before some more guests arrive at midday.'

When she spoke of guests, Steve did not grasp that Olive, long since deserted by a Sicilian husband who had made his way to New York without her, supported herself by running a boarding-house, largely frequented by Finns delighted to find someone who spoke their language. He merely assumed that she had some relatives or friends coming to stay with her.

He considered for a moment, head on one side. Then

reluctantly he said: 'Oh, all right. Just let me clean up and take these off.' He indicated the too tight, grease-stained dungarees lent to him by Beppo.

'You're an angel! I always knew you were an angel – from the moment I first set eyes on you.'

In the car, he asked her: 'Where did you get this MG? You don't see many of them back home, let alone in Italy.'

'From a boy-friend,' she replied. 'An English boy-friend. He was a darling. Teaching at the university here. He lodged with me. Then he got himself killed in an accident. Ghastly. The other driver was drunk,' she added. 'Bloody idiot! Thank God they sent him down for five years. In England or Finland he would probably have got off with a fine.' She took off the dark glasses, then replaced them. 'Fortunately they could patch up the car even though he, poor darling, was a write-off.'

'*This* car?'

She nodded. 'His mother came out here. Separated from her husband – a GP somewhere in South London. My pal was her only son. She didn't want the car, didn't even want to see it or talk about it. So . . .' She turned to him and smiled. 'I'm the only possessor of an MG in the whole of Sicily. Perhaps – who knows? – in the whole of Italy.'

They were now on the outskirts of the city. With none of Stefano's decisiveness on such occasions, she directed him down one street of tall, grey houses, many of them with washing dangling across their peeling stucco façades, and then down another. He all but missed the second turning because she was so late in warning him of it.

He stared at the brass plate, eyes screwed up against the

sunlight glinting off it. '*Pensione Gelsomino,*' he read out
with difficulty, pronouncing the G not soft but hard.
'*Pensione* is a kind of hotel, isn't it?'

'Let's say a boarding-house.'

'And you . . . ?'

'Yes, I run a boarding-house. For my sins. Or, rather, for
the sins of my second husband.'

'Was he called Gelsomino?'

'No, of course not, silly! In Italian *gelsomino* means
jasmine.' She mused. 'Mr Jasmine. No, that wouldn't have
been an appropriate name for him. Mr Stinkwort might
be better. When we first bought the house, there was a
jasmine bush over there. But it died long ago. I suppose I
should plant another. Do you know anything about
gardening?'

'Something. In Australia I created a garden around this
derelict house which I bought.' Suddenly he thought of
that garden. Digging and planting, he had been happier,
he now realised, than doing anything else in his whole life
– until he had started to work on the beautiful Bugatti.

A stout, elderly woman, a cloth wound round her head,
was lethargically swabbing the floor with a long-handled
mop. With a forced brightness Olive greeted her: '*Ciao*,
Maria!' The woman muttered a few words in return. As
Olive said something further in Italian, Steve became
aware that this hall, with its high, cobwebby ceiling and
lincrusta dado, was full of cats. One, black-and-white, with
an extraordinarlly large head and an extraordinarily
emaciated body, lay stretched out on a blue-and-white
deckchair. Some kittens were squirming at the teats of a
black queen in a corner. A majestic marmalade tom with
only one eye was grooming his tail on the stairs.

Olive turned to him. 'Here you see some – not all – of my family. People constantly throw their kittens over my garden wall. It's easier to do that than to drown them.' She began to lead the way down the hall. 'It was my family that first brought me into touch with Tilda. Now she's my closest chum. She does such wonderful work for animals in Sicily. And she's such a busy woman too, all those patients, never giving her a moment of peace. Well, neurotics are, by definition, selfish, aren't they? I have a lot of shortcomings but thank goodness I haven't an ounce of neurosis in my make-up. And that was just as well when I had to cope with that pig of a Sicilian husband of mine. My Finnish husband wasn't nearly so bad. He was just a bore.'

They had now reached a vast kitchen with, at its far end, an old-fashioned cast-iron range, clearly no longer in use since an electric stove stood beside it. A cast-iron trivet supported a number of battered, smoke-blackened cooking pans. Ranged on a shelf running almost the whole length of the room were innumerable dusty packets, jars and bottles. 'It's such a mess,' Olive said, reading his thoughts. 'But what's one to do? No time, no money. You don't want a job, doing some decorating, do you?'

Steve decided to treat the question as a joke. 'Oh, no, thank you. As soon as I've got the Bugatti back on the road I shall be off. I've so many more places I must see.'

'Stefano's going to miss you. Do you think you'll ever return here?'

He shrugged. 'I don't imagine so.'

'Poor Stefano.'

He sensed something which made him feel uneasy; but

he had no idea what it might be.

Olive crossed over to a wall-cupboard, opened it and dragged out a cumbersome hoover. 'Pre-war,' she said. 'It came with the house. Perhaps in a few years I can get a large sum for it as an antique. But meanwhile . . . if you can possibly get it to work again . . .'

'Let me have a look at it.' He took the hoover from her and placed it up on the kitchen table. 'Any tools?'

'There's a box of them somewhere here.' She began to search the cupboard. 'The tools were one of the things my husband failed to take. He got away with most of the silver.'

As Steve worked, Olive, seated opposite to him, with the hoover between them, continued to talk. 'I love Italy and even more I love Sicily. God knows why! The corruption here, the inefficiency – you've no idea . . . But it's far preferable to Finland or even England. I say that Italy is the country of creative chaos. Whereas Finland is the country of uncreative order. I fled Finland after three years of living there. Apart from being bored rigid by my husband, I loathed all that *asepsis.*' She gave a shuddering distaste to that last word. 'But England is hardly better.' She peered at what he was doing.

'Do you think you can get it to work?'

'I think so.'

'Oh, goody, goody! Well done!' She placed her hands on the knees revealed below her short, tight skirt and rubbed them vigorously with her palms, as though, on that day of summer, she was cold. 'I first came to Italy with a group of university chums – by then I was a mature student at London University – during the long vacation. And that was when I met my second husband. On a beach. He had this gorgeously muscular body – not unlike yours. One should never meet one's future husband on a beach. One is swayed by considerations which certainly do not guarantee a happy marriage. Apart from that gorgeously muscular body, he really had little to offer.'

When Steve had placed the hoover on the floor, connected its antiquated plug to an equally antiquated socket and coaxed it into an asthmatic wheezing, she cried out: 'It works, it works! You've got it to work!' She rushed to the door and called: 'Maria! *Maria! Vieni!*'

Maria, mop in hand, shuffled in, a resigned, dissatisfied expression on her face. But when she heard the vacuum cleaner, she hurried over to it with a grin. Taking its handle from Steve's grasp, she began to thrust it back and forth. '*Bene! Bene!*' she cried out. She turned to Steve: '*Bene, signore! Molto bene! Grazie, grazie!*'

'Well, that's the first time she's shown any pleasure in weeks. I put her recent bad temper down to her bunions. She was fine until the bunions appeared. I sometimes think that I should blow the expense and pay for her to have an operation.' Maria, having unplugged the hoover, now began to drag it off with her to the hall. 'Now what do I owe you?'

'Owe me?' He was puzzled.

'For your time and effort.'

'Oh, you don't owe me anything.'

'But I must owe you *something*. Don't be silly. After all, the labourer's worthy of his hire. Isn't that what people say?'

Embarrassed, Steve muttered: 'Please forget about it.'

'Well, that's awfully kind of you, but you do make me

feel . . . I'd never have asked you in the first place if I'd known you wouldn't let me pay . . . Anyway, if you refuse to take any money, then at least let me give you a drink. I have some Finnish vodka, given to me by the dreary couple who've just moved on. Or there's some whisky – I *think* – and of course all the usual Italian stuff. What's it to be?'

'No alcohol, thank you. I hardly drink at all. Some coffee perhaps?'

'Coffee? Of course! What a good idea. I'll have some coffee too.'

As they waited for the little espresso machine to come to the boil on top of the stove, the two of them sat on straight-backed bentwood chairs, facing each other across the kitchen table.

'You're very good-looking. Do people keep telling you that?'

Once again embarrassed, he laughed. 'Not very often!'

'Even Tilda thinks you good-looking. And she rarely notices men's looks. Unlike me! On the evening of your arrival, she remarked to me: "*Come è bello!*" In a whisper, in case you heard her. Not that you'd have understood the Italian, would you?' The machine was spitting steam. She got to her feet and returned with it to the table. 'She's a good sort, Tilda. What would Stefano do without her? That family used to be so rich, all those palaces, all those servants, all that rattling about the world. But now . . . Poor old S. hardly has two *quattrini* to rub together. What happened to all that money? Tilda's the breadwinner. And the practical one. Someone told me that Stefano didn't even know how to write a cheque. She handles all that side of things.'

'This coffee is good.' But in fact, like all Italian coffee, it was far too bitter for him.

'What do you make of this masterpiece he's supposed to be writing?'

Steve shrugged.

'It's rather pathetic really. Fancy shilly-shallying for a whole lifetime on a single book. I once met Graham Greene at a party given by that Dottoressa Moore over on Capri. One knew at once that there was a *real* writer. He got down to it – every day. He's created what is called an *oeuvre*. Hasn't he? But poor old Stefano . . .' She reached for the pot and poured herself out more coffee. 'I really sometimes wonder if that book exists. Perhaps, after Stefano's death, the only thing that people will find is a huge stack of sheets of paper, with nothing, absolutely nothing, written on them.' She gave a cruel bark of a laugh. 'How on earth did he and Tilda ever come to marry each other? A mystery – the mystery of human attraction! She'd have been much happier with someone else – a real man – and he . . . But I suppose in Sicily one can't lead the sort of life one can lead in Paris or London or San Francisco – or even Helsinki!'

Once again Steve felt an unease, but did not know its cause.

He got to his feet. 'I ought to be going. I must get back to the Bugatti.'

'Is Stefano paying you for all that work on the car?'

'Oh, no. No! Except that he's paying Beppo to allow me to use the garage.'

She stared at him closely. Then she laughed. 'The clever old bugger!'

'He and Tilda have been so kind to me. It's the least I

can do. Anyway, I'm *enjoying* the job. It's not like work. It's
– fun.'

'Well, if that's your idea of fun . . . Anyway, I think Stefano's
jolly lucky. He adores you,' she added.

'I – like him. A lot.'

Again there was that stare, followed by a laugh. 'Yes,
Tilda is right. You *are* a beautiful young man. And you
have such a wonderful innocence. No English or Italian
man of your age has it. Some Finns do. That's your great
attraction – apart from your looks. Your innocence.
Unworldliness, if you like.' She put a hand on his
shoulder. 'Don't lose it.'

He turned away, embarrassed, and also somehow
ashamed.

Yet another cat, a Siamese with eyes of the same pale
blue as his, sidled into the room and let out a screech.
Olive turned: 'All right, sweetie. I know, I know! You want
Mummy to give you your fish. But just wait a moment. It
isn't cooked and, before Mummy cooks it, she has to take
this kind gentleman back into town.'

'No, no. I want a walk.'

'It's *miles*, you know.'

'I love walking. And if I find that I've had enough of
walking, I can always hop on to a bus.'

'Are you sure?'

'Absolutely.'

'You've been a darling.'

Suddenly, standing on tiptoe, the cat rubbing itself
against her, she had put up her face and had kissed him
on the cheek.

As he trudged home in the heat – to walk like this, along

crowded pavements, with the din of traffic grinding in his ears, was entirely different from walking in the Bernese Oberland or over the hills at home – Steve traversed the conversation with Olive again and again. It was almost as though she had spoken to him in Lithuanian, a language of which he had learned some shreds from hearing his parents talk it to each other, and he was now trying to puzzle out what exactly she had been saying. In some obscure way, he decided, she had been making fun of Stefano. But the old man was always so courteous and kind to her on her visits to the house. Steve could not imagine his saying anything in the least snide or derogatory about her, or allowing anyone else to do so. It was ungrateful of her to speak of him like that.

Among many other things, Steve now suddenly recollected, she had said that Stefano 'adored' him. Had anyone else ever adored him? His father, no, certainly not. His mother? Well, yes, perhaps, in her detached, selfish way. Sue? He had thought so once, but now he doubted it. To be adored by Stefano made him feel uncomfortable. What had he done to deserve that adoration? He wanted to say to him, when next they were alone together: 'Look, don't imagine that I'm something I'm not. I'm just an ordinary bloke, a car mechanic, that's all. In Sydney, all over Australia, there are thousands and thousands of blokes not all that different from me.' To be adored made him feel as if some secret part of himself, hidden from the world, had somehow been penetrated and might even have been defiled.

As, footsore and sweating, he neared the garage, he saw a figure far off on the pavement ahead of him. He recognised the stoop, the frail swagger of the walk, the gold-topped stick, the panama hat with the wide red-and-white band. Often, when he had completed his stint for the day on the book, or when he just wanted a short spell of rest from it, Stefano would make his slow way from the palace to the garage. He must be on his way to the garage now. 'How are we getting on, Steve?' he would ask. It was always 'we', never 'you'.

Suddenly Steve did a thing with which he took himself by surprise. Instead of walking on towards Stefano with a smile of greeting, he turned quickly into a malodorous alley, hurried along it, and then turned into a road which led back in the direction from which he had come. What made him do so was something very strange. There had been a kind of click and rattle in his brain and then he had thought with horror: It's coming. It's coming. I mustn't let it come. *It* was the Needle Dream. He had never thought that it might come to him not in sleep but while he was out walking like this, down an alley crowded with cats and overhung with washing.

With a tremendous effort of the will – it was as though he were struggling to push away some vast object that had hurtled down on to him out of the previously empty sky – he at last succeeded in extricating himself.

Slowly, the Needle Dream faded, faded, faded, and with it, even more slowly, a strange, bitter, clinging, nauseating smell also faded.

IX

Tilda returned from Stefano's study. Under the red silk bandeau which imprisoned her copious blonde hair, there was an abstracted frown on her large, handsome face. 'He doesn't want to be disturbed. He's working. So he says.' She glanced at the man's large, old-fashioned Rolex watch on a gold bracelet on her wrist. It had once belonged to Stefano, she had told Steve when she had caught him staring at it, but he could not wear watches, they would not work on him, something to do with the electricity. 'Do you want to continue to wait for your tea?' Steve by now knew that she and Stefano never thought of their evening meal as 'tea'. Had she used that word to mock at him or out of some sort of misguided courtesy? She was a woman who, always hiding and hoarding her inner self, baffled and bewildered him.

'I don't mind waiting,' he said. 'I'm not all that hungry.'

She sat down on the sofa and took up the copy of *Oggi* which she had been reading. Then she threw it down and leapt to her feet. 'Oh, let's eat! Why should we wait any longer for him? I can put his food in the oven later.'

'I'll help you.' Now Steve also rose.

For the past two days Guido had been ill. He had insisted on getting up that morning to serve their breakfast for them, but had then all but collapsed while staggering in from the kitchen with the coffee. Sprawled out on a chair, trembling hand to forehead and his face a clammy, greenish yellow, he had seemed to be on the verge of tears at his impotence. Eventually Steve had helped him to his feet, with the tenderness which he always showed to anyone who was old or sick, and then, his arm around him, had conducted him, shuffling step by step, up the next flight of by now much narrower stairs and so to his small, bare, neat room under the eaves. Looking around that room, Steve had marvelled that the man should have spent a lifetime in the service of the family and yet have accumulated virtually no possessions. When he later told Tilda this, she replied: 'I suppose the answer to that is that he thinks that he possesses what we possess. That's why he looks after all our possessions so well. In a way, he's also looking after his own.'

Now Tilda protested at Steve's offer of help in getting their meal: 'No, no! I can manage. You've been working all day on that car.'

'And you've been working all day on your patients. I'd like to help you. Why not? I've nothing to do.' He might have added: 'I don't read, I hate music, and you don't have a television set.'

'You're a good boy,' she said, as they made their way down the corridor to the kitchen. 'You lay the table and I'll warm up the food. It all comes from that delicatessen next to the garage.' She laughed, turning back to face him as she did so. 'When I first married Stefano and we lived in the palace – the one that the Americans bombed – we had a cook and three assistants. Times change – and we change with them. Yes?'

When they had sat down, she in her usual place at one end of the table and he, at her direction, in Stefano's place at the other end, she unfolded her stiff, linen napkin and carefully tucked it in under her knees. Under the chandelier above her, her teeth looked unusually large, regular and white. Not for the first time Steve wondered if they were false.

She dipped a spoon into the bowl of minestrone before her. 'So you've never really got on with your father?' It was as though she were taking up a conversation interrupted only a moment before.

'That's right.'

'He was brutal to you? And to your sister?' These were things that Steve had told to Stefano, never to her. Stefano must have passed them on. Briefly Steve felt a pang at the betrayal.

'I suppose you could say that.' He was wary, as he never was when Stefano questioned him about his life or his family.

'Then you are looking for another father? Would you agree with that?'

He flushed, considered for a while, then shook his head. 'No. No, I don't really think so. Why should I want another father after my experiences with the first one? No.' Again he considered. The flush deepened, spreading down to his muscular, sunburned neck. 'No, I don't want another father. No.'

She leaned across the table. No doubt, he thought, this was how she grilled her patients. She was, he decided, a woman who liked the power gained from a knowledge of other people's secrets. 'Then what do you want?'

He resisted the temptation to say: 'To be left alone.' He raised a spoonful of minestrone to his mouth and slurped it up. At the sound, Tilda briefly winced. Then he said: 'What I want is . . . independence. Yes, that's what I want.

Not to – not to be beholden. To – to stand on my own
feet.'

'Then I wonder why you and Stefano get on so well.
Because what he wants is for you to be a son to him. Yes?
Am I right?' She played with the roll beside her, tossing it
in a palm, as though she were trying to assess its weight.
She smiled. 'I think that I am right. But you don't wish to
be his son.'

Steve said nothing.

'There's an impasse there,' she said. Again she smiled
and again she tossed the roll in her palm. Then she said:
'But you're a good boy, Steve. Yes, I really mean that. A
good boy. It is natural that Stefano should want you for his
son – the son I could not give him.'

Suddenly Steve wanted an end to all this probing. He
wanted to be out of the house, away from Palermo, alone
on a mountain, or on some vast, deserted plain, or on a
choppy sea.

'There is some beer for you on the sideboard. Stefano
reminded me this morning to order it for you. You see –
he thinks of everything for you. You are always in his
mind – on his mind?'

'Oh, thank you. But I don't feel like a beer. I'll just have
some water.' He reached out for the glass jug, its mouth
shielded by a piece of gauze weighted down by large,
multi-coloured glass beads at each of its corners.

For the next course, he had persuaded her that,
instead of heating up two chicken patties, she should
allow him to make them omelettes and a salad. He
worked at these things swiftly and silently, while, leaning
against a wall, she watched him intently.

She sliced a piece off her omelette with the side of her
fork and placed it in her mouth. She chewed meditatively.

Then she took up some of the salad and chewed on that too. She nodded in approval.

'You know how to cook.'

'Thank you. Omelettes have always been one of my specialities. One of my few specialities.'

'Before you go, you must cook us some of your other specialities.' She took another mouthful of omelette. 'Did you learn to cook from your mother?'

'Strangely enough, no. She's never been much of a cook. From my father.'

'From your father!'

'He once worked as a cook in a restaurant. In Lithuania, as a student. When he was studying the violin.'

Steve suddenly realised, for the first time, that the only occasions when his father had shown him any affection had occurred when the two of them, the man's face flushed with drink, the boy in an apron reaching almost to the ground, collaborated on the preparation of some meal. Curiously, at such times Steve's sister was never allowed to lend a hand.

Suddenly, after a long period of silence, Tilda asked: 'Is your father dead?'

'No, oh, no. He's only – what? – fifty-eight or nine. But he has a bad heart.'

'A bad heart? From what you've told me about him, I can believe that. Everything about him seems to be bad. And you still see him?'

'Yes. Sometimes. He had an operation – a bypass – not long before I left Australia.'

'And you still hate him?'

Steve shrugged.

*

When, after dinner, Stefano had still not appeared, Steve

became restless. Tilda sat in a deep armchair, its cretonne cover frayed, reading a copy of the *American Journal of Psychoanalysis* by the light of the standard lamp beside her. The wattage of all the bulbs in the house was extremely low. Steve had picked up an old copy of the *New Yorker* and was turning the pages, squinting down not at the text but at the cartoons, most of which seemed to him at worst unintelligible and at best pointless.

Eventually, with a sigh, he put the magazine down. 'I'm sleepy. I think I'll turn in.'

She looked at him, eyes narrowed. 'Yes, you look tired. Healthy, wonderfully healthy, but tired. You do so much. All that work on the car.'

'It's all but finished.'

As he rose to his feet, she said: 'Stefano will be sorry to miss you.'

'There's always tomorrow.'

'But how many more tomorrows? He must be asking himself that.'

Steve thought: You have a way of making me feel uncomfortable. So tolerant of physical discomfort, this was a kind of psychic discomfort which he hated.

'Sleep well!' she said, extending a hand, almost as though she expected him to shake it or even kiss it.

'Thank you. The same to you.'

Steve did not go to bed. Stefano had long since given him a key and so, when he had descended to the hall, he turned on an impulse not towards the door to the courtyard but to the door to the street. If Tilda or Stefano heard him either going out now or returning later, he would say that he had wanted a breath of fresh air.

He strolled, hands clasped behind his back and head

lowered, down towards the sea. Long before he reached it, he could smell its mingled odours of salt, oil and fish. Once there, he leaned on a stone parapet and stared into the mist which, clammy and warm even at this hour of the night, was rising off it. He could feel the mist in his throat and pricking at his eyes.

And you still hate him?

. . . The man who still has his son's good looks even though his once formidable body is now frail and emaciated, is sitting out in a deckchair in the exiguous, overgrown garden of the three-room bungalow on a spur of land sticking out into the sea. He can no longer properly run his building firm, and without him to chivvy and chase them, the three men in his employment, one from Greece and two from Lithuania, are negligent and, he suspects, also dishonest. In consequence, profits are small, and he is behind with his alimony payments to his former wife.

He listens, head laid back and eyes half-closed, to the far-off buzz of the motor bike which gradually intensifies to a roar. Steve appears over the brow of the hill. Even though his face is concealed by a helmet, it must be Steve. No one else would come here at this hour, late in the long summer evening.

'Hello, boy,' he calls out as, removing the helmet, Steve strides towards him.

'Hello, Dad! How're things?'

'Mustn't complain.' Endlessly he produces such phrases, learned long ago with relentless persistence from workmates, in a desire to show that he is no longer a Lithuanian refugee but one of them. 'Things could be better. What's going on in the city?'

'It's very hot. Far hotter than up here. That's about it.'

'And how are you, boy? Are you okay?'

'Yes, I'm fine.'

'Still with that actress girl-friend?'

'Yes, still with her.'

The father broods on that. 'I could do with a girl-friend myself,' he says. Then he adds: 'I wish I could get together again with your Mum.'

Steve shrugs.

'Did you tell her about me?'

'Yes, of course.'

'I wish she'd let bygones be bygones.'

Doesn't he realise how impossible that is, when the bygones are so terrible?

'She has her own life?' the father pursues.

'Yes. That's right.'

'With someone else?'

'No. By herself. She was always independent. You know that, Dad.'

'Like you. You got that independence of yours from her.'

Steve wants to say 'I had to be independent. I couldn't depend on either you or her.' But instead he suggests: 'Shall I make you some tea or coffee?'

'You could get me a drink.'

'Okay. What would you like?'

It is many months since the father was able to brew his home-made wine. 'There's a bottle of Scotch inside. That'll do. As I always have it.' That means neat. 'Help yourself to some too – or to anything else you can find.'

'Thanks. I'll make myself some coffee.'

The father used to taunt the son about his

abstemiousness – 'You're a real sissy, aren't you?' – but he
does not do so now. Instead, his still handsome face
flushed by the light of the setting sun, he smiles to
himself with a strange, self-mocking kind of desolation.

As Steve waits for the water in the electric kettle to boil
before making the instant coffee, he thinks of Sue. The
reason he has come to visit his father is that she is visiting
her father. Her father asked her to be his hostess at a
dinner party at which the guest of honour will be a
colleague from MIT – 'Steve won't be offended at not
being asked, will he? It won't be his sort of scene, he'd
only be unhappy, a fish out of water.' Sue told Steve that
she would stay with her father overnight – that way she
could drink as much as she wanted without having to
think of the drive back home. Steve feels a sudden
longing for her, a physical ache somewhere behind his
sternum and in his loins.

The father sips at his whisky, holding the glass against
his lips with emaciated, trembling hands. Steve looks at
those hands. 'Do you still play the violin?' He feels a
transient nausea as a memory surfaces, unbidden, of a
man in his underpants, his chest and even his back
covered in thick black hair, playing a sentimental waltz by
Strauss, Lehar or Waldteufel to the child whom he takes
such pleasure in tormenting.

'Not since the bypass. Don't seem to have the taste for
it any longer. Maybe, when I'm feeling really better . . .'
Suddenly he brightens. 'Today I made my own bed. Took
my time about it but I made it. Didn't wait for Flora.'

'Flora?'

'The one from next door, the widow. You remember?
You met her last time you were here. She's a good sort.

She keeps telling me I don't have to pay her. But of course I do. I don't want to be beholden. I've always hated to be beholden. She's a good sort but, Christ, is she ugly! I think that she might fancy a bit of nooky, she's more or less said it to me once or twice, but I'd have to be really desperate *and* blind to go for that one.' Suddenly all the old brutality is revealed and Steve, who had previously been feeling tender, even affectionate, recoils at it.

'None of the old girl-friends can be bothered with me. Well, Hilda comes up now and then. But she's too taken up with those grandchildren of hers – a dreadful pair of brats, worse than you and your sis at that age. She wanted to bring them along with her but I said Not on your bloody life. I've enough to contend with, getting over the op, without them running about the place, making a din.'

The sun, large and lurid, is beginning to sink. 'Would you like me to wheel you to the bluff?' Each time that he pays a visit, Steve does this for his father. Together they look out over the sea. Once, when they were doing so, his father pointed and said: 'Far over there is Singapore, and beyond that Thailand, and beyond that India, and beyond that Turkey, and beyond that Austria, and beyond that Poland . . . Strange to think that I visited all those places in order to come to this hell-hole.'

Steve fetches the wheelchair and all but lifts his father, who begins to breathe stertorously, sweat breaking out on his deeply lined forehead, into it from the deckchair.

'Away we go!' That is what Steve's mother used to say when she wheeled him off to the shops in his push-chair. Steve has never heard his father say it before.

Suddenly, as Steve is pushing the chair up the hill, he thinks: Why the hell am I here? He owes the bastard nothing. At that, rage, hot and bitter, surges through him. The rage gives him a demonic energy; he pushes the chair faster and faster.

When it jolts on a particularly high tussock and all but tips over, the father cries out: 'Hey! Hey! What's the hurry? Are we late for something?'

Only for your funeral, Steve thinks.

'I love it up here. Trouble is I can't make my own way up and, apart from you, there's no one to push me. Flora is such a tiny little thing – all skin and bones.'

The father looks suddenly benign and serene as he gazes out over the wide expanse of the sea, dotted here and there with minute, tufted islands. Its farthest extremity has become a glowing bar, a gigantic gasfire radiant, in the light of the setting sun. Steve realises that, if he and his father have nothing else in common, at least they have in common this love of the natural world, so much superior (Steve has long since decided) to the human one.

Steve is standing behind the wheelchair. Then, all at once, he feels a terrible temptation. It would be so easy to give the chair a push, a gentle push, not a shove, just a push, which would precipitate it down the grass slope and over the cliffs. He would find some convincing reason for the accident. He would say that the brake must have failed; or that his father, in his despair at his condition, had himself released the brake, while Steve was standing elsewhere. There is no one up here now. No one will contradict him.

But he can't, can't! He can imagine such things, has often done so ever since, as a small child, he cowered in terror of his father in bed or behind a sofa or at the far

end of the garden; but he cannot do them, it is not in him
to do them.

His father says: 'You know, Steve, during these months
of illness I've had a chance to think about the past. I really
mucked things up. Perhaps I should never have left the
old country, Communism or not. Once I'd left, nothing
really went right.'

'Dad, what are you talking about? You made a great
success of your life over here. You came with nothing and
now . . . You have the business, your investments, the
house.'

'Do you really think that I made a success of my life?'
The father stares bleakly at the sun as it dips below the
horizon. 'I don't. I've – I've so many regrets. Things done,
things not done. I fucked it all up.' He looks, his face
ashen and crumpled, as though he were about to burst
into tears. In his lap, his right hand twitches
uncontrollably.

Then, all at once, Steve's whole being is flooded not, as
so often in the past, with rage and hatred, but with love.
Why should he love this horrible old man? Yet, at that
moment, he does, he does. He puts his hand on his
father's shoulder. He has never before touched him in
love; nor has he ever felt his father's touch except when it
descended, cruel and malevolent, to hurt him in some
way. Then he bends, the light of the setting sun
reddening his forehead and his cheekbones under those
pale blue eyes which now also seem to glow red.

He puts his lips to his father's dry cheek. He kisses it.

His father jerks his head away and then turns it back to
look up at his son, first in amazement and then with a
piteous gratitude.

'Steve – why did you do that?' he asks.

' . . .*Buona sera.*' The voice behind him was light, metallic. Steve swung round and took in the squat, slightly preposterous figure in a wide-brimmed black hat and a voluminous black cloak reaching almost to his black patent-leather shoes. How could he bear to wear that cloak on a night as hot as this? It reminded Steve of the way in which Tilda dressed.

The man smiled, a gold tooth glinting in one corner of his mouth. 'You remember me, Steve? You are Steve – yes?'

Steve nodded. 'Yes, I remember you. Of course.' It was the playwright with whom he and Stefano had shared a restaurant table a few days before.

'You are enjoying our city?'

'Very much.'

The Italian gave a twirl to his cane – not unlike Stefano's, except that it had an ivory head, of a grinning monkey, instead of a plain gold one. 'Our city has much to offer – if one knows where to look for it.'

'I'm not really fond of cities. I prefer the country.'

'You are a country boy. I can see that.'

Steve turned away, about to take his leave. Sensing this imminent departure, the Italian quickly asked: 'And how is our old friend? The Prince,' he added, when he received no immediate answer from Steve.

'Very busy.'

'Busy?'

'On his book. His novel.'

The playwright gave a squawk of derisive laughter. 'I've never known anyone be so busy doing *niente, assolutamente niente* – nothing, nothing at all.'

Indignantly Steve said: 'He's working very hard. Sometimes early in the morning, often late at night. He's getting to the end.'

Again there was that squawk of derisive laughter. 'For as long as I have known him – ever since I had the *temerita* – the temerity to speak to him when I was a student and he was giving a lecture on *Tristram Shandy* – the first modern novel, he said, I remember that, I remember that well – he has always been nearing the end. That was before the War, long before.' He edged closer to Steve, eventually to lean on the balustrade beside him, so that their elbows almost touched. Steve could smell on him a sweet, sickly odour. Sweet-pea? He thought so but could not be sure. 'That day when I meet you – Stefano is cross with me. But that waiter is happy. People like to be told that they are beautiful. The one thing' – he raised a finger and wagged it back and forth – 'that you must never tell no one is that he is ugly.' He turned his simian face to Steve. 'I tell you now – you are beautiful. Are you offended? Are you angry? Of course not! You are pleased. Yes?'

Steve scowled. 'I must get back.' He made a show of looking at his cheap watch on its canvas strap. 'It's getting late. And I must get up early tomorrow.'

'Late!' The Italian looked at his own flat, gold disc of a watch. 'It is not yet *mezzanotte* – midnight. Why do you not come to see my apartment? It is there – over there!' He pointed with his cane. 'Five minutes, no more. I wish to know more about your country. You can tell me. Next year, in Australia, in Sydney, they perform one of my dramas. Maybe we meet? Why not? Maybe you show me your country, we travel together?' He gave an arch grin, then, his mouth suddenly thinning and his eyes narrowing: 'Unless, of course, the Prince persuades you to stay on in our Palermo.'

'I'm afraid there's no chance of that.' Steve began to move off. 'Now I must get home . . . Goodbye.'

Behind him the light, metallic voice rang out: 'Goodbye, Steve. *Ciao! Buona notte! Buon divertimento!*'

Then Steve once again heard that squawk of derisive laughter.

X

Over breakfast, Steve told Stefano: 'I think I've come to the last day.'

'The last day?'

'Of work on the car.'

'But, Steve, that's wonderful!' Then with a catch of disappointment, as though he had only just realised all the implications of what Steve had said, Stefano added: 'I never thought that you would be finished so quickly.'

'There was actually less – far less – to be done than I'd thought. Someone maintained that car extremely well over the years.'

'Well, it wasn't me. It was Aldo. My father's chauffeur. He loved that car even more than my father loved it. He never stopped washing it and waxing it. Poor Aldo!' He sighed. 'He was' – Stefano hesitated for a word – '*seduced* by the bull-frog . . . Mussolini,' he explained, seeing the look of incomprehension on Steve's face. 'During the War, he became one of Mussolini's drivers. And when they killed Mussolini and that Petacci woman, they killed Aldo too. But at least they didn't string him up naked for everyone to kick, punch and spit at. How could Aldo have been so stupid? How could so many Italians have been so stupid?' He lifted his coffee cup in both his hands and peered down into it.

'Would you like some more coffee?' In the absence both of Guido, now in hospital, and of Tilda, already closeted with an early-morning patient, it was Steve who had prepared the breakfast for Stefano and himself.

Stefano waved his hand in refusal. Then he said: 'I say that Aldo was stupid. But what was I? I was a coward, a coward. I – I – what is the English phrase? – I kept my head down all through those terrible years. I have no courage, Steve. I have stoicism, yes, a little stoicism, I can endure things, but courage – no!' He rose slowly to his feet. Steve noticed how his shabby but well-cut suit was hanging on him and how the collar of his striped black-and-white shirt – made in Jermyn Street, he had boasted to Steve, though to the Australian that meant nothing – seemed at least two sizes too large. Clearly, he was losing weight drastically. 'I must return to my book. I think . . . I think . . . perhaps we shall both finish our tasks on the same day.' He smiled, suddenly happy.

'You mean . . . ?'

'Well, there is polishing to do. And things to add – and subtract, no doubt. But, yes, I think that at last, at long last, I have finished. All that time, all that thought, all that effort. Was it really worth it? That's the question.' He began to walk unsteadily towards the door, putting out a hand now to a table and now to a chair for support. The Pekinese called Mimi, clearly his favourite, waddled behind him. Then he turned: 'And your great task – was that worth it?'

'Oh, yes, yes!' Steve spoke with total sincerity. 'Absolutely. I loved working on that car. It's something I'll always remember. I don't think I'll ever work on another car like that.'

'Why not?'

'Such cars don't exist back home.'

'You could work on it for ever – if you would only stay here in Palermo.'

Steve treated the suggestion as a joke. He laughed: 'I could hardly do that!' Then he realised, with a shock of dismay, that Stefano was in earnest.

'Why not? You could stay on here with us, you could make this house your home.'

'What would I do to earn a living?'

'A living?' The way the old man spoke the words gave the impression that to earn a living was something of no importance. 'Well, you could go into partnership with Beppo. Or you could open a garage of your own. Or . . . Or . . . Oh, there are so many things you could do! I've often told you – you're *intelligent.* You've never had a proper education but you have the ability to learn. The other day I heard you saying something to Beppo in Italian, and you said it perfectly – almost no accent at all. Oh, do give it some thought. Stay with us!'

'What about my mother?'

'Bring her here to be with you. There are so many rooms empty in this house. We could make her an apartment in it. No, no, I am being serious,' he cried out, once more returning to the breakfast table. 'Good things only happen in life if one *makes* them happen.'

'I don't think my mother would think living in Sicily a good thing.'

'In any case – you could visit Australia from here. Every year, if you wanted. Is that so difficult?'

'It's expensive.'

'But I could help you with that.'

It was all too absurd. But this was not a game that Stefano was playing, although Steve had first thought that it was. The old man was perfectly prepared to create the flat or to pay for the journeys back and forth. Steve rose to his feet. 'Well, I'd better get over to the garage. Beppo promised to give me a hand, provided I was early.'

'Oh, Steve . . . Think about what I have said. You will, won't you?'

An inherent, unquenchable honesty forced Steve to say: 'Thinking about it can't possibly change my mind. I'm sorry.'

'Oh, Steve, Steve, Steve . . . There is so much I want to say to you and yet, somehow, somehow I can't, I can't. I am more English than Italian in that I have this inability . . .' He pressed his hand against his heart. 'Here.' Then painfully he stooped and patted Mimi, who in response looked up at him with huge, bulging, grateful eyes, wagging her tail. 'You have no difficulty in showing what you feel. Do you, *carina?*'

The bitch wagged her tail even more frenziedly.

When the last of the spokes of the huge wheels had been given their final polish, the leather-covered seats had been carefully replaced, and the engine had then been kicked into roaring life, Beppo and Steve stood side by side, staring in silence at the Bugatti.

'A beauty!' Beppo exclaimed, having learned that from Steve.

'*Che bellezza!*' Steve exclaimed, having learned that from Beppo.

Beppo threw an arm around Steve's shoulders and hugged him to him. Steve resisted his instinctive urge to pull away from the contact of another body on his.

At that moment Beppo's plump, attractive wife, with her fringe of thick black hair over eyes that constantly

flashed with amusement or anger, clicked out from the
office in her immensely high-heeled, scuffed red shoes,
their straps pinching her ankles. She said something to
Beppo in Italian. Steve heard the word '*soldi*', which by
now he knew meant 'money', and, twice repeated,
'*avanza*', which was strange to him. Beppo muttered
something and shrugged.

Then Beppo's wife turned to Steve. Having worked in a
canteen for the American forces in the immediate
aftermath of the War, she spoke a little English, in a high,
breathless voice, totally unlike the one, strong, deep and
nasal, in which she spoke Italian. 'He no pay nothing. *Il
principe*. No pay no money.' She rubbed fingers and
thumb together. 'You speak. Yes? You speak to *principe*. No
good, no money. You speak!'

'Okay. Don't worry. He must have forgotten. *Forgotten*!'
Steve shouted the last word, in that common belief that,
if one says something loud enough, it will in the end get
through to a foreigner.

He crossed the garage forecourt, intending to walk the
short distance back to the palace. Then an idea came to
him. He opened the car door, clambered in, placed the
key in the ignition. Once again the engine roared into
life. Expertly he manoeuvred the monster in the narrow
confines of the garage and, just failing to graze a Morris
Minor on one side and a Peugeot on the other, ventured
out into the road. Beppo and his wife were waving him
farewell. But he did not notice them. He was full of an
extraordinary sense of power and an extraordinary
exhilaration.

Stefano later said that he had, in some strange way,
already known that Steve would be coming in the car.

As the Bugatti boomed down the road and then screeched to a halt at the kerb – Steve was driving it with a joyful recklessness, not with the sober caution with which he drove the Fiat – the old man was peering down from the window of his study, Mimi standing beside him. Behind, on his desk, were piled the many pages, covered in the minuscule, unjoined letters of his hand, of the novel just completed. There must still be many more scratchings out and many more additions, he had decided, but nonetheless he felt as if, after a lifetime of arduous sailing, with shipwreck always threatened, he had now at last come home to port.

At precisely the same moment that Steve, having raced up the steps, entered the hall, Stefano appeared at the top of its staircase. The old man extended both arms in welcome. 'We have both come to the ends of our journeys on exactly the same day!'

In his euphoria Steve experienced a fugitive impulse to run into those extended arms. He laughed. 'Yes, yes! But your journey has been so much longer and harder than mine.'

'Oh, don't remind me of it! At least we can both say "*Nous avons fait un beau voyage.*" '

'Come again?'

But Stefano did not translate for him. Instead, he hurried down the stairs, at such a speed that Steve put out a hand, terrified that he would fall. Like a rabbit, Mimi loped down behind him. Once down, the Italian turned to the bitch: '*Mi dispiace, carina.* You must stay here – with your mistress.' The dog squatted and looked up at him with an expression of reproach. 'Mimi understands! She always understands!' he exclaimed to Steve. Then he lowered a hand and stroked the dog's head.

Out in the street, Stefano circled the car, head tilted now one way and now the other. 'She's so beautiful,' he said. 'I'd forgotten how beautiful. Only a few of that model were made – and most of them for royalty. How could I have ever abandoned her in that garage?' Then he turned to Steve: 'But what am I to do with her?'

'Impress everyone in Palermo by driving about in her.'

'But how am I to drive about in her if you go? I should be terrified of driving such a monster. And so would Tilda. She is even terrified of driving that horrid little Fiat.'

'You could sell her, I suppose. You'd get a lot of money for a car like that.'

'*Sell* her – after all the work you've done on her? Oh, no, no!' Then he cried out: 'Now we must celebrate the two achievements – your achievement, my achievement. Let's drive somewhere for lunch and drink champagne and enjoy ourselves.'

'Perhaps the Princess would like to come too?'

Stefano hesitated, clearly not pleased with the suggestion. Then he said: 'I'll go up and ask her. But she did tell me this morning that she had an extremely busy day. Meantime, why don't you fetch your bathing costume?'

'My trunks? Are we going to swim?'

'*You* are going to swim. I am afraid that my swimming days – like my dancing days – are over.'

Steve ran to fetch his trunks and then waited for several minutes in the hall. When, at long last, Stefano returned, it was to announce, with obvious relief, that, as he had thought, Tilda was far too busy to come with them. '*La poveretta* – she works so hard. Why, why? She should enjoy life more.' Steve remembered what Olive had said about Tilda being the breadwinner.

Stefano had brought a silk scarf with him. It flapped crazily in the wind, like a flag on a flag-pole, displaying its Sulka label, as the car ravenously devoured mile after mile of the serpentine Corniche. From time to time he laughed from the sheer pleasure of travelling at such speed, and Steve then joined in the laughter.

'Whe-e-e-e!' Steve bent low over the wheel, as the car hurtled round a particularly sharp bend. 'This engine must be doing at least 48,000 rpm. In the thirties this type was the absolute tops.'

'This is how we used to travel in my father's time – except that Aldo never drove as fast or as dangerously as you.'

'Do you want me to slow down?'

'No, no, of course not! I was thinking that, if one had to die, what better way to die than by driving off the road in your company in this car.'

'Thank you! I don't want to die.'

'Well, as I told you in the museum, the archer's arrow isn't ready for you yet – not for a long time. But for me . . .'

Later, Steve remembered Beppo's wife's vehement complaints about the money owed to them by Stefano. 'Oh, by the way, Beppo's wife was rather going on about not being paid.'

'Not being paid? Not being paid for what?'

'For my use of the garage.'

'*Bello, guai!* What bloodsuckers! That's the Sicilian peasant for you. Because they are peasants, for all their present prosperity and airs and graces. Do you know how that family escaped from their village? My father, my dear, generous father, gave them – not lent them, mind you, *gave* them – the money to buy that piece of land, that piece of land on which they built that garage. That land, in the middle of the city, is hugely valuable now. But do they show one ounce of gratitude? Of course not! Instead they badger me to pay them for the use of a corner of their garage for a week or two.'

After this outburst, he stared moodily down at the hands resting in his lap for several seconds. Then he burst into laughter. 'When we return home, I'll give you the money and you can take it over to them. *Noblesse oblige.*'

Stefano had planned that they should go to a seaside village where, before the War, he and Tilda had spent a few weeks, she taking long walks with her dogs in the surrounding hills and he wrestling (as he grandiloquently put it) Jacob-like with the angel of creation. But looking down on this place, before turning off the Corniche, he cried out: 'No, no! We can't go there!' Where there had been a barrier of stunted trees, there now stretched a long, low hotel, all matt concrete and glittering glass, and, beside it, a car-park crammed with cars and coaches, the overhead sun flashing off their roofs. 'Drive on! On!'

Stefano rejected another village – 'Spoiled, spoiled!' he cried out in horror and dismay – before finally declaring: 'This will do! Yes, I remember this little place. Probably we can find no champagne. But the beach and the sea are perfect for you – hardly a soul – and I myself can sit in the shade of those trees over there.'

Leaning back against a tree, a trembling hand raised to his forehead to shield his eyes from the glare, even though he was also wearing his panama hat, Stefano

watched Steve as he swam out and out, until he was
almost lost to sight. When at long last the Australian
returned, Stefano said: 'How well you swim! I thought you
would swim away for ever – eventually to land in Sardinia
or even Greece. I can't swim, you know.'

'Not at all?'

'Not at all. Isn't that shameful? The only times when my
father ever got angry with me were when I refused to go
into the sea. Once, at Biarritz, he tried to drag me in and
I screamed and screamed and screamed, until my mother
stopped him. My cousins made terrible fun of me for not
being able to swim – just as they made terrible fun of me
for not being able to throw a ball overarm.'

As Steve dried himself, Stefano never ceased to watch
him. Then the old man said: 'Henry James was right.
Youth *is* the Sacred Fount. You know, I feel so much
better when I am with you. I almost forget that I am
dying.'

'But you're not dying.'

Stefano shrugged and the corners of his mouth went
down. 'We are all dying. But I am dying more quickly than
most people.'

Amazingly, the owner of the little trattoria beside the sea
was able to produce a bottle, not of Asti Spumante or
something similar, but of French champagne; and, even
more amazingly, the champagne was chilled. Stefano
raised his glass, the bubbles of the champagne glinting in
the sunlight. 'To our twin achievements. To us.' He put
the glass to his lips, sipped, sighed. 'Nectar!' Then he
laughed. 'Actually champagne is terribly overrated. I'd
much rather have a good Chablis.'

'We now have a rather good Australian champagne. So my father tells me. He likes to think himself an expert.'

Stefano pulled a face. 'Champagne can only come from Champagne. It can't come from Australia. Your father cannot be so much of an expert.' Then, realising that he had snubbed Steve unnecessarily, he added: 'But there are now some very good Australian wines.'

Their coffee before them, Stefano lolled back in his wicker chair. 'I'll always remember this day. Perfect.' He raised his hand, removed his panama hat, to reveal a red line, like an incision, on his pale forehead, and placed the hat on the table between them. 'We Sicilians do not care all that much for the sun. We have too much of it. But today – I don't know why – it is good to feel the sun on my skin.' He peered into the face opposite to him. 'Do you always have that tan?'

'Yep. I spend so much of my time out of doors. Gardening, swimming, trekking. But, as I said, the sun isn't always good for one.'

'I think of you as a creature of the sun. So bright – and glowing – and warm – and – well . . .' – he raised both hands, palms upwards, in the air – '*sunny*!' He burst into laughter.

At that moment, the proprietor of the little trattoria hurried out to where they were sitting. Excitedly he called in a high-pitched, nasal voice, long before he had reached their table: '*Principe! Principe! Di nuovo! Una catastrofe!*' A cascade of Italian then poured out of him.

A look of horror gradually darkened the old man's face. He turned to Steve, who had understood nothing: 'This is terrible.' A moment later, he said: 'It is Marco. He is dying, maybe dead.' He turned back to the excited

Italian beside him. '*Si! Si!* . . . *Come?*' Then he once more turned to Steve: 'He heard it on the radio. Marco has been shot. His daughter too.' He staggered to his feet. He put out a trembling hand, grabbed his glass, and drained it in a single gulp. 'We must go there. Now! At once!' He reached into his jacket for his wallet, but the proprietor put up a hand '*Dopo, dopo!*'

Steve had never driven at such a speed in his life, now bullying the Bugatti up some precipitous hill (Stefano had insisted on a series of cross-country short-cuts) and now coaxing its vast, raging bulk around a series of hairpin bends.

'Those brutes,' Stefano muttered. 'It must be them. But what did he do to offend them? What, what? They have no morals – no consciences – no gratitude.'

'Do you mean . . .? You think it was the Mafia?'

'Of course! Who else? Unless it was some act of vendetta. Marco has had to do some terrible things for them. That's the way it is – once you are one of them. So perhaps . . . *Chi lo sa?*'

On their previous visit to the empty palace, the three of them had been alone in a silence broken only by the scrape of their feet on gravel, the creak of ancient wood as they trod on a rickety stair or loose board, and always, inside or out, by a racket of birds such as Steve had never heard before in his life, even during his treks through the Blue Mountains or Kosciusko National Park. Now everything was different. The drive was full of police cars, private cars, radio and television trucks. As the Bugatti roared up, innumerable people turned, hands raised to shield their eyes from the sweltering sun, and gazed at it. Recognising Stefano, a dumpy, heavily moustached police officer, gold braid glinting on his tight jacket and oversized peaked cap, stepped forward. '*Principe!*' he exclaimed in astonishment. He raised an arm in a stiff salute. Later, Stefano was to explain to Steve that this police officer was the son of one of the family *contadini* on a remote estate, rarely visited by him and Tilda, in a far corner of the island.

The two men conferred. Then more and more people joined them. The babbling of excited voices rose to a crescendo. No one paid any attention to Steve, who, looking about him, suddenly saw something dark and glistening under one of the high ground-floor windows. It was some seconds before he realised that it was blood. That must be where Marco had been shot down.

The officer, Stefano at his side, pushed his way through the crowd, manhandling anyone who did not move quickly enough, towards the palace. He pointed at the glistening, star-shaped stain. Stefano halted in his tracks, stared, then cupped a hand over his mouth, as though he were about to vomit, and gave a little whimper. The officer halted and delivered, with an abundance of histrionic gestures, what appeared to be a lecture. Stefano nodded and nodded. Then he turned to Steve: 'That's where he died. There! Just there. That's his . . .' He turned his head away, unable to bring out the word 'blood'.

As they entered the palace, the officer leading, with Stefano and Steve beside him and three uniformed policemen bringing up the rear, there were angry cries and mutterings as no one else in the dense, struggling crowd was allowed to follow. Clearly Stefano, with none of the political power or the wealth of his ancestors, nonetheless still enjoyed some feudal privileges.

The body had been laid out, on a sheet of polythene, on the long table which stretched almost all the way from one wall of the dining-room to the other. Draped over it was another sheet of polythene. The two policemen, seated uncomfortably, rifles resting across their knees, on straight-backed bentwood chairs which Steve remembered from his previous visit, lumbered to their feet. One opened his mouth to say something and, at once, as from a blow-torch, a smell of garlic enveloped everyone.

Stefano stared for several seconds at the shrouded form. Then he tottered, put out a hand and placed it on Steve's shoulder for support. That hand had so often gone out almost to touch Steve and then had failed to do so. This time it not merely touched him, it rested on his shoulder for many seconds. Steve could feel, he did not know how, an urgency and terror pulsing from it into himself.

Stefano removed his hand and staggered forward. Fingers of his right hand now twitching at one corner of the polythene covering, he looked at the officer. The officer shrugged, pulled a little face, which caused his huge moustache almost totally to cover his full, blubbery mouth, and then nodded. Slowly, tentatively, Stefano pulled back the sheet, as though he were coaxing the dressing from a wound.

He gave a little wail. Half of Marco's face had been blasted away, and the fingers of one hand were shattered, clotted blood stuck to them so that they looked grotesquely distended. Stefano bent over the body and at the same time the officer's and Steve's gazes interlocked. The officer's face expressed both amazement and shock. Stefano had put his lips to the forehead of the corpse, just to the left of where it had been shattered into pulp. Then he turned away, head bowed and eyes shut.

Steve went across to him, tried to ease him round to face him. But with remarkable strength in one so frail, Stefano kept turning away. Realising that he wished to be left alone in his grief, Steve released him. Again Steve's gaze interlocked with that of the officer. The officer raised his shoulders in an eloquent shrug; then, no less eloquently, he raised his eyebrows and pursed his lips.

Eventually, a large monogrammed handkerchief pressed with one hand to his mouth and trailing down his chest, Stefano stumbled out from the gloom of the house into the glare outside. Everyone stared at him, motionless. Then a reporter rushed forward with a microphone. '*Principe! Principe! Un momento per favore! Un momentino!*'

Stefano staggered on.

Now the reporter shoved his microphone at Steve. Excitedly he said something in Italian. Steve put out a hand and pushed the microphone aside.

By the Bugatti, Stefano, now in some measure of control of himself, turned to the officer. They exchanged a few words.

'His daughter is in the city hospital. They took her there by ambulance. Her arm is injured, that is all.' Stefano opened the passenger-side door of the car. 'We must go and see her. Her name is Katerina,' he explained, with what Steve thought a strange irrelevance. '*Andiamo!*

Come!'

Steve walked round to the driver-side door and pulled it open. The handle was still too stiff, tomorrow he must see to that, he told himself, just as no doubt tomorrow Stefano would decide that something equally trivial needed adjusting in his novel. Stefano was saying goodbye to the police. Again the reporter with the microphone approached, and this time Stefano cried out angrily to him: '*Niente! Niente! Lascia mi stare!*'

As the car veered round one hairpin after another in its descent, its two occupants were silent. Steve was bewildered by the extremity of the grief which he had witnessed. What had happened was tragic, horrible, disgusting. He himself would never forget, he knew, that first sight of that shattered face, the clotted blood almost black against the grey-white of lacerated skin and shattered bone. But Stefano had reacted as though the dead man were not merely the custodian of one of the family palaces, but a brother or a son.

In a faint, parched voice, Stefano broke the long silence. 'Poor Marco. Why did he ever get mixed up with that crowd?' He put his hands between his knees and then closed the knees, gripping the hands in them as in a vice. His jaw began to tremble, his body to shake, as though he were freezing on that day of extreme heat. 'I warned him. From the start. Many times after. I remember him as a child, when I was still a student. I remember him as a young soldier, doing his military service. I remember him . . .' He gulped. 'It was I who gave him that job. I am godfather to Katerina – his daughter. I paid for his wife to go to Rome for treatment for her leukaemia.' He shook his head. 'No good. She died. Died quickly. Only twenty-seven.' He bowed his head, his panama hat tipping forward and covering his forehead. Then his fragile body was convulsed with violent sob on sob.

Steve glanced sideways at him. He wanted to do something but he did not know what.

In the end, his eyes all but closed as he stared at the dazzling road ahead of him, and his usually generous mouth tensed into a line, he merely drove on.

Two heavily moustached *carabinieri*, with knobbly, tobacco-stained fingers and long, thin legs stretched out before them, were seated on guard outside the hospital room. They at once recognised Stefano, lumbering to their feet and deferentially greeting him as he approached, a doctor and a nurse ahead of him and Steve behind.

Marco's daughter had been segregated at the end of a corridor. As they had walked down it in a silence broken only by the squeak of the nurse's rubber-capped heels on the worn linoleum, Steve attempted to translate what was written on now this door and now on that – *Farmaceutico, Pelle e Venere, Urologia, Ostetricia.* Clearly there were no wards here.

An extremely high, narrow window illuminated what appeared to be a room created by taking a slice out of one much larger. Under the window stood an iron truckle-bed and on it lay Marco's daughter. One arm, heavily bandaged, rested outside the sheet. Her eyes were shut in that extraordinarily beautiful face which Steve had seen gazing at him out of a window of the derelict palace. The face, with its greenish sheen, looked bloodless. For a

moment he thought: She's dead! Then, at the sound of
the door clicking shut, she opened her eyes and stared,
with what was all too obviously terror, at the four visitors.
Steve was sure, as her mouth opened, that she was about
to scream. But instead she emitted a small, choking wail.
Then she began thrashing about on the bed, grinding
her teeth, her eyelids fluttering. The nurse, a large,
middle-aged woman, marched across, bent over, and said
something in a loud, scolding voice. The girl became still,
as though paralysed, staring up at the nurse with eyes
wide and dark with terror. Steve knew that state of
paralytic terror all too well. He himself had so often
suffered it as a child.

Now Stefano joined the nurse. '*Katerina . . . Senta, cara
. . . Mi dispiace* . . .' His voice was gentle, loving, consolatory,
as it crooned the words. He might have been the girl's
father or her grandfather as he bent over her.

Her response amazed and shocked Steve. She jerked
up, her face transformed by what could only be loathing
and disgust. She began to scream what was clearly abuse,
on a single high, piercing note. At this verbal onslaught,
as though invisible hands were beating at him, Stefano
recoiled, tottered, seemed about to fall over, until he put
out a hand and gripped the bedhead. The girl continued
to scream.

The nurse, once again approaching the bed and
leaning over the girl, shouted something angry. Then the
doctor, with his stooped shoulders, nicotine-stained
fingers and white, bushy moustache, intervened, soft-
voiced, placatory, calming. Katerina subsided back on the
bed, turning her face sideways to the wall so that it was no
longer visible. With a movement of the head, the doctor

indicated that they should leave. At that, the three men shuffled out of the room, leaving the nurse behind them. In total silence the trio once more traversed the corridor and then descended the staircase to the ground floor.

When the doctor had left them, with a few mumbled words of comfort, Stefano sank on to a wooden bench outside one of the wards. An ancient woman, in a nightdress and with grotesquely tangled grey hair, was already seated on it, gnarled hands clasped in her lap as she rocked back and forth while singing tonelessly to herself. Steve remained standing.

'What was all that about?'

Stefano stared ahead of him, mouth half-open and tip of tongue caught between lower and upper teeth. He did not answer. He did not look at Steve.

'What was all that about?' Steve repeated the question.

Stefano shook himself, as though out of some long reverie.

'Hate is strange. I mean, the – the genesis of hate. Even stranger than the genesis of love. I never knew before that she hated me. I did so much for her – her mother – her father. But she hated me, she hated me all along.'

'But why on earth should she hate you?'

'Why do people hate each other? Why do people love each other? One falls in love, one falls in hate.'

'But there must have been some reason.'

Stefano shrugged. 'Maybe. It is all so complicated. Maybe.' He began to struggle to his feet. 'Maybe I could find some explanation. Something to do with her father . . . her mother? . . . Who knows? . . . I must try to think about it . . .' Again he shrugged his shoulders. Lowering his head, he frowned down at the floor.

Then: '*Andiamo!* Come! *Come!* I cannot stand the noise being made by this crazy old woman.'

Suddenly he sounded brisk, impatient, irritable.

XI

Steve was later to realise, guiltily, that he had chosen the worst of all times to break to Stefano the news of his imminent departure.

Slumped and largely silent, the old man had pushed aside, after a few mouthfuls, the plate of lasagne which Tilda had set before him.

'What's the matter?' she asked with unusual sharpness. 'Isn't it all right?'

He waved a hand in the air. 'It's fine,' he muttered. 'Nothing wrong with it. It's just . . . I have no appetite.'

'You've got to do something about this constant loss of weight. Not eating is so *stupid.*'

'Oh, don't, don't *nag* at me!' he cried out. 'Can't you see I'm upset? Do use some imagination.'

'I can understand that Marco's death has been a shock to you,' Tilda retorted in a cool, cutting voice. 'But I'd hardly have thought . . . You're carrying on as though it were some family tragedy.'

Stefano buried his face in his hands. 'If you had seen his body!' he groaned.

Ignoring him, Tilda turned to Steve. 'What about some more lasagne?' She pointed to the sideboard. 'Why not finish it off?' She got up from her seat, strode down to the other end of the long table, and snatched up Stefano's plate. As though knowing what she was about to do, the dogs crowded around her. She stooped and lowered the plate to the floor. 'What a waste!'

'No, no, no!' Stefano wailed. 'Not between meals! And lasagne is not good for them. You will give Mimi diarrhoea.'

'I hate waste,' Tilda retorted. 'You know that. If you didn't want the dogs to have the lasagne, then you should have eaten it.'

Steve had rarely known Tilda and Stefano talk to each other in this fashion. Usually they maintained an elaborate, almost artificial politeness.

Later, as they drank the coffee which Steve had prepared in the old-fashioned Cona machine, Stefano brightened a little. 'Now that we are both free of our tasks, we must think how best you can see the rest of the island. One of my favourite places is Adrano. I'd like to show you that. It's what used to be called Adranum in classical times. There's a wonderful eleventh-century castle there. The Bourbons made a gaol of it.'

At this point, Steve, having become increasingly restless, broke in: 'It all sounds terrific. But I'm afraid – if I'm to see all I want to see – I'll have to get a move on.'

In consternation, Stefano gazed at Steve. In turn, Tilda gazed at Stefano, and then, lips parted, lowered the *petit point* on which she had been working.

'A *move on?*' Stefano repeated the phrase as though it were one he had never heard before. 'What exactly do you mean?'

'Well . . .' Steve had already realised that he should have deferred any talk of leaving Palermo until the next day. 'My schedule is tight. There are so many places . . .'

Indignant, Stefano cut in: 'But you haven't seen a *tenth* of what you must see in Sicily. Not a tenth. You'd be mad to leave now.'

'If I had unlimited time . . . But I haven't.' Suddenly Steve was bubbling with a panicky claustrophobia. If he was not careful, this old man would imprison him here for ever, using gratitude, pity and guilt as the means to do so. At all costs, he must not give in. 'In fact . . . I think that tomorrow I must start enquiring about the cheapest way to get to Sardinia.'

Stefano stared gloomily into the empty grate beside him. Then he shook himself. 'Perhaps I might accompany you to Sardinia.' All at once, he smiled; he liked the idea, now that it had come to him. 'Why not? The book is finished – or as good as finished. I need *un petit changement de décor.'* Steve, stunned, did not know how to respond. 'And after Sardinia . . .? What do you have in mind?' Stefano pursued. Once again Tilda, lips pursed and an angry flush in her usually sallow cheeks, lowered her *petit point* as she stared across at him.

Steve shifted uncomfortably in his armchair. 'Greece, I think. If I can get some sort of boat across.'

'Oh, Greece, Greece! I'd love to show you Greece. The ambassador is a friend of mine. I played with him as a child and then, years later, we met again in England. He's such a nice man. And very intelligent. I'm sure he'd put us up.'

Steve shook his head. 'It's awfully good of you. Really. But . . .' How could he explain it? 'You see, your way of travelling is not my way. It can't be. I like travelling rough, I prefer to travel like that than any other way. And I like travelling alone. That probably seems odd to you but I'm I'm a loner. I once read somewhere – or heard somewhere, I don't remember – "Two's company, three's a crowd, but one is a wanderer." That's what I am – the one who's a wanderer. I like to be alone, I like just to wander without any plan and without any commitment.' Oh, how could he, how could he explain it? Tilda and Stefano were looking at him as though he were crazy. 'Perhaps it's something to do with my childhood. So often being locked in my room by my father, even being tied to my bed. So often being told by him what I must do. I have to be *free*. Free of any obligations. Not committed to anyone else, or even to a programme.' He looked from one to the other of them. 'Do you understand that? Or does it seem quite crazy?'

Stefano gazed back at him in stony despair. Tilda nodded. 'Yes, I think I understand.' Then, after a pause, she said bitterly: 'Really I envy you. It must be wonderful not to be attached to anyone or anything – not really attached.' She went on: 'I've come to divide all people into dogs and birds. The dogs, once you have tamed them or attracted them, will do anything you ask of them, they will be faithful to you, they will never desert you. The birds, beautiful creatures, fly into your garden, they pick up whatever crumbs you throw out for them, they sing a beautiful song and then . . . they leave you! Without any pang of sorrow or regret or guilt. Sometimes they may fly back again. Often not.' She stared across at him, baring those teeth which might or might not be false, in a smile that was almost a grimace. 'You are a bird, Steve. Definitely – you are a bird.'

The next morning Steve ate breakfast alone. Tilda had already eaten hers, he surmised from the used crockery and cutlery at her usual place. Was there any significance in the fact that Stefano had still not appeared? Was he ill? Offended? Hurt?

Back in his room, Steve, always tidy and methodical, began to lay out his things prior to packing them. From a line which he had put up between two pipes in the bathroom, some of his T-shirts and Y-fronts dangled. He felt them appraisingly. They were not yet dry. Soon he must go down to the harbour and enquire about boats across to Sardinia. He was determined to find the cheapest passage possible. Should he buy some farewell present for Tilda and Stefano? At once he dismissed that idea. He had so little money for the long journey still ahead of him. He was determined not to fritter it away.

There was a loud rap on the door and, before he could call out, Tilda had opened it, the three dogs behind her. Quickly she surveyed the things laid out on the bed. Then in a loud, challenging voice, she said: 'So you really mean to leave tomorrow?'

'Yes, I'm afraid so.'

She remained standing in the doorway, as though she thought that to enter further might somehow compromise her. 'Stefano needs you,' she said. 'I hate to say it or even think it but he does. Badly.'

He shrugged. He felt angry at what he saw as an essentially base appeal. Then he said: 'I'm sorry.'

'Now that the book is finished, it's essential that he has that exploratory operation. It may show that there's nothing seriously wrong, but all the tests so far' – she gazed intently at him – 'suggest the opposite. Ever since that bronchoscopy, I've been begging him to have the operation. In these cases, it's madness to delay.'

'But I don't see . . . how can I . . .?'

'Of course you don't see! But you must believe me. He *needs* you.'

'But why? What can he need me for?'

'Your presence. He says that your presence gives him – hope. Courage too, he says, the will to go on, to live.' Suddenly she took a step into the room. One of the dogs, having followed her, began to snuffle at one of Steve's boots. 'I don't understand it any more than you do. But that's what he says. He has this belief in you – in your goodness, he says.' She gave a bitter, little smile, a large hand raised to the braid encircling her head. 'To be frank with you, I must tell you that I see nothing exceptional in your character, none of that *spirituality*' – she gave the word an ironic emphasis – 'which my husband finds. You're very handsome certainly and you're very helpful and you have a lot of charm, but that's the sum of it. For me. For him, however . . .' Now she sat down on the bed, pushing aside a pair of jeans to make room to do so. 'So I come with this appeal to you. Please stay on until the operation is over and we know – we know for certain – what the future holds for him.'

Head lowered, Steve considered. Oh, how he hated all these clamorous demands on him, this conscripting of him to do a duty he had no wish to do, this impinging on the freedom more important to him than any obligation to anyone, however close. He shook his head. 'Sorry. I'm terribly sorry. But I've already stayed in Palermo far longer than I intended. My plan was to be here only for a day – for two at most.'

Tilda got off the bed. Suddenly he felt apprehensive. 'So you refuse to listen to the plea of an old man who's been so kind to you – who needs you so much – who may be dying?'

Steve said nothing, head lowered.

She strode to the door. Then she turned. 'Do you know what I think of you, Steve? Do you?'

A sense of dread lurching up through him, he looked across at her. Involuntarily, he gave a weak, silly smile.

'I think you're a shit!'

At that, she walked out, slamming the door behind her.

XII

What Steve would most have liked to do the next morning would have been to shoulder the backpack and slip out of his room and the house long before either Tilda or Stefano had risen. But, after all their kindness to him, that was, he had decided, out of the question.

The previous day, after his confrontation with Tilda in his room, had been an exceptionally difficult one. He had had to eat both a midday meal and 'tea' with them. Tilda had been virtually silent, turning over the pages of one of her many foreign journals of psychoanalysis while she ate. Stefano had gamely tried to make conversation, but it was clear that the task was as onerous for him as it would have been for him to carry Steve's backpack in his present state of health. Alarmingly, while Steve was pouring out the after-dinner coffee from the Cona, the old man was suddenly convulsed by one of his coughing fits. The rasping and racketing went on and on, while Steve stood over him, the glass globe of coffee in one hand, and Tilda, her medical journal lowered to her knees, looked anxiously across. Then with an agitated, scrabbling movement, Stefano plucked one of those huge, heavily starched, monogrammed handkerchiefs of his from the breast-pocket of his white linen jacket, now hanging with a pathetic looseness on him, and pressed it to his mouth. A red stain began to spread across it.

'*Stefano! Cosa c'è?*' Tilda pointed in horror. '*Sangue!*'

'*Niente! Niente!*' The coughing had stopped. He folded
the handkerchief, folded it again, yet again, and then
slipped it into the side pocket of his jacket. 'It happens
sometimes,' he went on in English. 'It used to happen
when I was a boy. But I survived.' He gave her a weak
smile. Then he held out his cup for the coffee, tilting his
head up to give Steve another weak smile and muttering:
'Thank you, Steve, thank you.'

Earlier that day, Steve had walked down to the harbour
in search of a passage to Sardinia, not on one of the spick-
and-span boats which regularly transported people, most
of them tourists, between the two islands, but on
something less elegant and cheaper. Those whom he
consulted despatched him back and forth from one boat
or shipping-office to another, but for the next day, the day
on which he had resolved, with all his innate obstinacy,
that he must leave without fail, despite any further pleas
that his host or hostess might make to him, there was
nothing.

Discouraged and thirsty, he went into a little café for a
glass of mineral water. Three old men, tumblers of wine
at their elbows, were playing what seemed to be some
form of three-handed whist, flinging down their cards
from a great height on to the formica-topped table, with
whoops of glee or derision. At another table two filthy,
paunchy, balding men in grease-stained dungarees and
sandals were carrying on a conversation in a language
which Steve knew was not Italian.

Steve placed himself at a table near to this couple. One
of them, the one sitting opposite to him, eventually
noticed him, grinned to reveal an almost toothless
mouth, and then raised a hand to his forehead in a

parody of a military salute. 'Hey, boy!' he called out.

'Hey!' Steve returned the jocular salute.

'You American?'

'No.' Steve smiled and shook his head. He felt far more at ease with this grubby, grinning, obese man than he had ever felt with Stefano. 'Australian.' The man shook his head in incomprehension. 'Australian,' he repeated.

'Okay, okay!' It was clear that the man had not understood. He pointed with a forefinger at his own chest and announced: 'Me Greek.' Then he pointed at the man opposite him. 'Him Greek. Brother. I speak little English. Sister in Nea Yorkie. Marry GI. You visit Greece?'

'Not yet. But I hope to do so.'

After that it was easy. The two men were off a caique, which they owned. They had brought a cargo of sheep to Palermo, they were taking back one of fruit. By a miracle they also had to pick up another cargo in Sardinia. Sure, sure, they could take Steve. He could pay them what he thought fair. Okay?

Steve nodded: Okay.

'I hardly slept a wink last night.' Was Steve being unduly insensitive in interpreting the words as an oblique accusation? 'I felt utterly exhausted. But somehow I just couldn't drop off . . . My mind in such a whirl . . . *And* I took a pill – two in fact.'

Steve felt a searing pity for the old man, as he looked at him over the used breakfast cups and saucers. But he was also filled with the determination not to yield to these increasingly pathetic appeals.

Tilda had already left, before Steve's arrival, to deal with another of those patients who came to see her before going on to their jobs. Steve hoped that she would still be occupied with some patient, this one or another one, when he made his departure. He shrank from saying goodbye to her, though he knew that that was cowardly.

'This is a sad day. I've become so used to your youthful, sunny presence.' Why did the old boy have to go on and on this way? 'I wish, oh how I wish, I could make you change your mind.'

'Sorry. No chance of that, I'm afraid. I've already booked on this Greek boat.' In fact, he had not yet paid anything to the Greeks. He could all too easily just not turn up.

'And you leave soon, well, almost at once? I'd have so much liked to have shown you at least the Palazzino Cinese – the Chinese pavilion – in the Parco Favorita. Marvulgia designed it – a miracle of chinoiserie. But' – he sighed deeply – 'I can see that's not to be.'

'I must be down at the harbour by ten. Otherwise they'll just sail without me.'

'And how are you going to get to the harbour?'

'Oh, walking. It's not all that far. Or I could take a bus, I suppose.'

'Let me take you in a taxi.' Before Steve could make any reply, the old man went on: 'I'd really like you to drive us both down to the harbour in the fiery chariot. The Bugatti,' he explained, seeing Steve's look of incomprehension. 'Our last ride in it together. But then how would I get it back? I certainly would never dare to drive it. Even that horrid little Fiat is now beyond me.' The corners of his mouth sagged downwards in despair. 'I wonder if I'll ever drive again. Somehow – it's not a question of strength but of quickness of reaction and of *will*. You drive so well.

Marvellously. Even at those terrific speeds the day before yesterday I felt totally safe.'

'It was lucky I wasn't caught for speeding.'

'If you had been, I'd have produced a bribe of the right size and that would have been the end of the matter.' He gave a derisive chuckle. 'I don't suppose you can bribe your police in Australia. I often wonder what it would be like to live in an essentially *honest* country. England was like that when I spent those years there. But they say that now . . .'

As they waited in the hall for the taxi to arrive, Steve said: 'I'm sorry not to have seen the Princess to say goodbye to her. Would you – would you please say goodbye to her for me? And thanks. Many thanks.'

At that moment, having deserted her patient, Tilda appeared at the top of the stairs, looking down at them. 'Are you leaving, Steve? So early? I heard your voices. Why didn't you come to – ?'

'I didn't want to interrupt your session.'

She advanced down the stairs, one large, white hand clutching the rail while the other raised her long skirt, so that she should not trip on it. She was smiling with a sweetness which Steve knew, knew at once, could only be genuine. All the vicious rancour of the previous day was clearly in the past.

'Today you look more handsome than ever,' she said. 'The angel that troubled the waters.'

Steve remembered that Stefano had once used that phrase to him. Stefano must have repeated it to Tilda. 'No angel, I'm afraid. Just a very ordinary bloke.'

'Can't a very ordinary bloke be an angel?'

She came close to him, then put up her arms, the gauzy

sleeves of her long, shapeless dress falling away to reveal them in all their plumpness and whiteness, and slowly placed a hand on each of his shoulders. He tensed, tried not to recoil. How he hated to be touched!

Gently she put her lips first to one cheek, then to the other. '*Buon viaggio,*' she murmured. 'God bless!' Then, with a small sigh, she turned away and began to mount the stairs.

The taxi moved by fits and starts through the heavy morning traffic. At first Stefano sat slumped, looking extraordinarily tiny and frail, the fingers of one hand resting on his lips, as though to impose a reluctant silence on himself. Then he moved the hand. Briefly it hovered butterfly-like, as so often in the past, and then, as never in the past, it settled lightly on Steve's hand. 'Dear Steve,' he said. 'I have arranged that tomorrow I go into the hospital. Tilda wanted me to go to Rome or Zurich but I prefer to be here – in my own city. I am not afraid, not even of death. In a strange way, I do not know how, you have given me courage.'

Steve did not know what to reply. The old man's hand still resting on his, he gazed out of the window. Then he asked: 'Isn't that the main post office?'

Stefano peered short-sightedly. Then he nodded. 'Yes. Why? Do you wish to see if there are any more letters for you?'

'It might be a good idea.' The previous night, Steve had had a long and confused dream about Sue – he had arranged to meet her by the caique, she had failed to turn up, then, far off, he had seen her walking with someone, an Italian, who had looked from the back, tall, broad-shouldered and shambling, amazingly like Marco.

Waking, he had only been able to sleep by masturbating while thinking of her. Now she was still in, or on, his mind – as Tilda had told him that he was in, or on, Stefano's. Perhaps by now a letter had arrived from her? 'The next poste restante is in Athens. And I told people not to send anything there until next week.'

'Your arrangements don't seem foolproof – far from it!' Stefano gave an indulgent smile.

'What else can one do when one is constantly travelling?' When the taxi drew up outside the post office, Stefano opened the door beside him and began to struggle to get out.

'Oh, you don't have to come with me. I can manage. I'm sure the clerk must understand some English. He must be used to tourists calling for their mail.'

'No, no! I'll come with you, I'll come. You never know. You may need some help.'

Steve wanted to shout at him: 'I'm not a child. You don't need to take care of me. I've been travelling alone for more than a month. I can look after myself.' But restraining himself, he slowed his pace to accommodate Stefano's as, side by side, they mounted the cracked marble steps. Though there were fewer than a dozen of these steps, at the top the old man, blue-veined hand pressed to breastbone, was gasping for breath. '*Un momento!* Just one second. Let me get my breath back. Oh, Steve, you've no idea how *hideous* it is to grow old. I don't recommend it.' He gulped for air, mouth wide open to reveal the costly gold inlays at the back of his mouth, and then gulped again.

Steve was about to approach the clerk, a different one from the one on the previous visit, but Stefano pushed in front. As always when he spoke to his social inferiors, his tone was imperious, peremptory; and, as always, the social inferior, in this case a middle-aged man, seemed not to resent it.

After a long search among the pigeon-holes, the man returned with a single letter. But it was not for Steve but for a Mr Stiebel.

'I'm sorry, Steve. You still do not have your letter. Perhaps in Athens . . .'

'I didn't really think there'd be one.' But he had hoped, oh, how much he had hoped, that there would.

'Poor Steve.' Stefano had gauged the full extent of his disappointment.

Back in the taxi, Stefano said: 'Do you think that you will write to me?'

'Of course.' Then with that natural and often brutal truthfulness of his, Steve felt impelled to go on: 'But don't expect a letter too soon or too often. I'm a terrible correspondent. I have this difficulty in writing, I've never been any good at it.' (Once, when he had written a letter to Sue, absent in Perth on a theatrical tour, she had demanded on her return: 'Is *this* your idea of a love letter?') 'And don't expect a long letter, will you?'

'Any sort of letter will be fine.' Stefano thought for a while, looking out of the window beside him. 'Then he turned his head: 'You could telephone,' he said. 'Reverse the charges, of course. Please do that. Telephone. If you reverse the charges, then it won't cost you anything. I don't want it to cost you anything.'

'Yes, I could telephone.' Steve was reluctant.

Stefano pulled out his worn, crocodile leather wallet and drew out his card. He held it out. 'On here I have written the number of the Blue Sisters. That is where I'll have my operation. I'll be there for, oh, at least a week. You could telephone me there. Yes? Just to tell me that all is well with you, that you've arrived safely in Sardinia. Otherwise' – he gave a sad, self-deprecatory smile – 'I will worry about you. It's in my nature to worry. I can't help it. Sorry.'

'I'll telephone,' Steve said.

Soon, he was leaning forward to instruct the driver where to find the caique.

'Is *that* what you are proposing to sail in?' Stefano demanded, pointing across.

'Yep. That's it.'

Stefano was alarmed. 'It must be ancient. It doesn't look at all seaworthy. Oh, Steve . . . The straits can be very rough, you know.'

Steve laughed. 'Oh, I think I'll be all right.'

Stefano was once again struggilng to get out of the taxi. He had half opened the door when Steve put out a hand and pulled it shut again. 'Please don't get out. Let's say goodbye here.'

'But I'd like . . .'

'*Please!* I'd prefer it that way.'

Briefly Stefano stared at him. Then he gave a small shrug and a shake of his emaciated body. He raised a fist and gave a little, discreet cough behind it, totally unlike that convulsive, never-ending coughing which Steve had heard so often before. 'All right, Steve,' he said in a small, resigned voice. 'As you wish.' He gazed intently into those arctic blue eyes with his own dark-shadowed, almost black ones. Then he said: 'I wonder if we'll ever meet again.'

'Why not?' But Steve knew that it was highly unlikely.

'*Casa mia è casa Sua.* My home is your home. Remember that. And remember that I am always here to catch you if you fall.'

Tilda had commented more than once to Stefano that Steve found it difficult to say thank you. He hesitated now, again finding it difficult. Then he said : 'Thank you, Stefano. Thank you a lot. It's been terrific, really terrific.' It was the first time that he had ever called Stefano by his Christian name.

Again Stefano stared at him in that searching, unnerving manner. Then he said: 'As always there is so much I want to say to you, and I can't, can't. Do you remember what Cordelia says to Lear?' How could Steve remember? He had never seen the play, never even read it. Stefano tilted his head back and closed his eyes as he recited: ' "Unhappy that I am, I cannot heave my heart into my mouth . . ." That's me, that's me exactly. Oh, if only I could heave my heart into my mouth. But I can't. So much that ought to have been said in the course of my life has gone unsaid.'

Steve clambered out of the taxi. He did not think of offering to pay for it. He had now come to accept, after an initial reluctance, that when they were together it was always Stefano who would pay. Had Stefano not said more than once that he *enjoyed* paying? 'Goodbye. And again – thanks, thanks a lot.'

Without waiting for any response, Steve then turned away and bounded up the gang-plank. Once aboard, he looked back. The taxi was already moving off. He raised a hand in a final salutation, but Stefano, his head tilted forward and his panama hat obscuring his eyes, did not respond.

Steve sat perched up in the stern, gazing out over the tranquil, grey-blue water, here and there shimmering with the rainbow colours of an oil-slick. *I've made it. I've got away. I'm free!* He was filled with a tremendous exhilaration, similar to that which used once to fill him when, leaving home behind him, he would set off, a resolute, beautiful child, with long legs and an already muscular torso, for the hills where he could wander for hours all alone.

One of the two brothers approached, expertly riding the roll of the caique as the swell kept tipping it sideways. In one fist he carried a greasy tumbler half-full of what looked like water.

'*Ouzo!*' he said with a grin. 'Good. Very good.'

Steve, who had so often refused wine when it had been offered to him by Tilda or Stefano, reached out eagerly for the tumbler. 'Thanks,' he said. 'Thanks.' He raised the tumbler. 'Cheers!' Then he took a gulp of the raw, aniseed-flavoured spirit.

XIII

Over and over again in the dormitory of the youth hostel, the American with the bandeau holding his long, blond hair in place, would bend over his guitar and sing 'The House of the Rising Sun'. The repetition maddened Steve, who lay out on his narrow, sagging bed, in nothing but his Y-fronts, from time to time irritably brushing away one of the plump flies which settled on him. The two men were alone in the elongated, stone-floored dormitory, empty beds stretching on and on beyond them. The American's companion had disappeared into another dormitory, with a group of Swedish schoolgirls. But for her, Steve might have supposed that the American, with his long, carefully tended hair, his long, carefully tended nails, his sinuous movements and his soft, high-pitched voice, was a poofter. He did not wish to be alone in the dormitory with a poofter. He had had a disturbing and embarrassing experience with one, a Japanese, in the shower-room of the youth hostel in Paris. It was that same night that he had had the Needle Dream, for the first time on his journey of a lifetime.

'How about turning in?' Steve eventually said. 'It's been a long day.'

'How about it?' The American went on playing for a while. Then he rose to his bare feet, put down the guitar on the empty bed beside him and said: 'I'll put out the light.'

In the dark, the American said: 'From appearances, you seem a decent sort of guy. That's the word. Decent. One can't imagine you doing anything shameful or wicked.' He spoke with a playful irony.

They went on talking for a while. The American said that he was from San Francisco; that he and his sister (so his companion was not after all his girl-friend, as Steve had thought) were bumming around the world; that they had been staying with some 'loaded, really loaded' friends of their parents in Rome before coming on to Sardinia. Then suddenly his voice slurred and he fell silent. Steve realised that he was asleep.

Steve, arms behind his head, stared up at the ceiling. The light, reflected off the sea beyond the window, shimmered across it. In that reflected light he could see the once restless flies now looking like small scabs on the cracked, dingy plaster. Somewhere close to him a mosquito emitted its attenuated wail, then drifted off. He was glad that he was taking his daily Paludrine tablets, as advised by an Australian doctor whom at the time he had thought to be too fussy.

One can't imagine you doing anything shameful or wicked. Well, not wicked, no, Steve thought. I'm not a wicked person, as my father is – or, at least, was. But, in a rare mood for self-laceration, he decided that, yes, it had been shameful of him to have hurried away instead of staying with Stefano at a time when he was about to undergo an operation which he all too clearly dreaded and when he might – yes, it was possible – soon be dead. Stefano, for whatever unfathomable reason, had, with a passionate urgency, wanted and even expected him to stay; and he had then denied the old man that solace, thinking only of the next lap of this hectic journey of a lifetime. Basically I'm selfish, he told himself. Yes, I'm kind and considerate and self-sacrificing – as people so often tell me – provided that nothing of real importance is involved. But essentially I'm ruthless. As he came to that conclusion, he asked himself the question which he often asked himself at moments of despondency and discouragement in the years ahead. Unless there was an accompaniment of sexual passion, as with Sue, was he really capable of loving anyone? He so often described himself as a loner. By that, did he not really mean that he wished to be alone to love himself, without the distraction of having to love someone else as well?

Restlessly he tossed from side to side on the bed, all at once aware that the hard pillow beneath him smelled nauseatingly of cheap hair-oil. But his inner restlessness was far more acute than this outer one, which was merely an outward manifestation of it. He thought: I betrayed him. Then he thought: He's the first person I've ever really betrayed. Next morning, he decided, he would telephone.

But the next morning, after a night first of that self-questioning wakefulness and then of erratic, febrile dreams, he encountered the American's sister at early breakfast. In the empty dormitory, the American still slept on, his guitar resting on the unmade bed beside him and his high-heeled, red leather boots resting below it. The girl reminded Steve of Sue. She had the same air of health and stamina, the same high colour, and the same long reddish-gold hair. She was wearing a light cotton blouse over pale blue cotton trousers, and through the blouse he could see her nipples as dark shadows. She talked animatedly to him, from the moment when she carelessly scattered cornflakes from their packet over the table – 'Oh, clumsy me!' – to the moment when, her breakfast finished, she got up saying: 'I'd better go and wake Max. How he loves to sleep! It's such a waste of life.' Her own name was Beth, she had already told Steve.

It was then that Steve should have telephoned, as he had planned to do. But instead he placed another teaspoon of instant coffee in his cup, poured on the hot water, and then sat before it, staring out of the window at the sea. It would be a beautiful day, and this was a beautiful place, unspoiled and wild, and she was a beautiful girl.

Beth returned with Max, who was sleepily rubbing his eyes and whose long, narrow feet were bare. He grunted, no more, when Steve handed him the cornflakes packet, and grunted again when Beth, having made him some instant coffee, put the cup down before him.

Beth began to ask Steve about himself. 'You're a *car* mechanic! Well, that's something, that's really something.'

Steve smiled. 'It's nothing,' he said.

'But car mechanics are really useful members of society.'

'So are painters,' Max said. Steve was later to discover that Beth was a painter.

'Not in the same way. At best we painters can only hope to please a tiny, educated minority. But car mechanics ...' Steve was soon to conclude that Beth, unlike Sue and unlike Max, was not all that bright. But that did not matter to him.

'And what are you, Max?' Steve asked.

'At present' – Max rubbed the lid of one eye with a forefinger and then gave a lazy, self-indulgent smile – 'I'm searching. I don't want to commit myself to any one way of life.'

I don't want to commit myself. It was something that Steve himself would often say. But he meant something different by it.

'How do you survive?' Steve asked.

'How do you mean, old boy?' Max put on a jokey upper-class English accent.

'What do you do for money?'

'Oh, I sponge off my Daddy.' He made the admission with smiling insouciance. Steve could not conceive of sponging off his own father. 'Fortunately he has a lot for the sponge to mop up.'

Beth leaned across the table. She put her fingers around Steve's bare upper arm. 'Boy! Do you have some muscles! You should make Max feel ashamed.'

'Yeah, I'm a weakling, I admit it,' Max said.

Steve stared at those two dark shadows under the flimsy cotton blouse. The elderly man in charge of the hostel had passed in and out of the dining-hall and Steve had totally forgotten to ask him about telephoning Sicily.

Soon, the telephone call still not made, Steve and the two Americans were setting off on hired bicycles to some caves which the Americans' guidebook said should on no account be missed but which, in the event, proved to be hardly worth the long pedal up one hill after another under a relentless sun.

Later, they found an empty beach. 'Let's have a skinny dip,' Beth proposed; and then before either of the two men had acquiesced, she had begun eagerly to strip off her clothes. For a moment Steve averted his eyes; but as she revealed more and more of her healthy, firm body with unheeding, unprovocative naturalness, as though she were doing the most ordinary thing in the world, he began to watch her with intensifying pleasure.

Max had squatted under a tree. Then he lay back and closed his eyes, and almost at once fell asleep. Beth ran down the beach to the sea and Steve, having removed his clothes, followed her. They swam out and out, the water warm and soapy on their bodies. She swam close to him, then, treading water, brushed her lank hair away from her face. She laughed, revealing white teeth against her sunburn. She laughed again, with the kind of joy that Steve himself had only experienced when trekking alone in the wild, and then, all at once, threw her arms round his neck. He held her close, feeling her breasts and thighs against him. She wriggled closer, put down a hand.

'I've never done it like this before.'

She laughed. 'Well, I have! What does the car-sticker say – "Surf-riders do it standing up"? I'm good at surf-riding. Apart from painting, it's my greatest talent.'

Later, they joined Max under the tree. He had opened his pack and had been preparing a joint. 'This is the first time for me,' Steve confessed, sucking on the pinched wad of paper when it was handed to him. 'I feel nothing,' he said later. But that was not true. He felt a numbing, effortless calm gliding, a huge, somnolent snake, within him. 'How was the swim?' Max asked and Beth answered: 'Terrific.' Brother and sister exchanged a long look. Steve then knew that Max knew.

Beth drew a sketch pad and some crayons out of her

brother's pack and got to work. When Steve eventually inspected what she had been doing, the criss-cross lines and interlocking circles bore, for him, no resemblance to the scene in front of her. He was bewildered but said nothing.

Over lunch in a café that was little more than a thatched shed with some tables set out before it, he told them of how, the next day, he was planning to take the caique which had brought him from Sicily to Sardinia and travel on with it to Patras. He had made friends with the two brothers who owned it, they were a terrific pair, so kind, so funny.

'What a brilliant idea!' Max said. 'We could come with you.' He turned to his sister. 'Couldn't we?'

'Why not? Egypt was to be our next stop, but why not Greece instead?'

'The boat's far from comfortable,' Steve warned.

'Oh, who cares?' Beth pushed a hand up through her long, reddish-gold hair and fluffed it out, in an effort to dry it. 'We've had so much comfort in our lives. A little discomfort is good for us. Isn't it?' she appealed to her brother.

'You bet it is!' He began to roll another joint.

Suddenly Steve thought of his day by the sea with Stefano. The old man, his book finished, and he, his work on the car finished, had both been so happy. That was the first time in his life that he had drunk champagne, real champagne; and that was the first time in his life that he had been master, complete master, of a car of such ferocious power. Once more, guilt overwhelmed him. Tonight he must, must ring. He must find out what had happened.

'You're very thoughtful all of a sudden,' Beth said. 'Not just thoughtful, you look sad,' she amended.

Max drew deeply on the joint held between the middle and forefinger of one of those beautifully kept hands of his. Then he squinted down at it. '*Omne animal post coitum triste,*' he said.

Steve had no idea what that meant and was too embarrassed by his ignorance to ask. If Stefano had said something unintelligible like that, he would immediately have queried it.

The telephone was on a wall just outside the kitchen, from which came a constant clanging and clattering and the sound of women shouting at each other and screeching with laughter. There was a strong smell of disinfectant rising from the concrete floor and another, more pleasant smell of what was being cooked in the kitchen.

Steve could barely hear the operator and, though the director of the hostel had said that she would certainly understand English, she did not do so. Eventually, after several attempts at communication, during which he shouted more and more loudly and with greater and greater exasperation, Steve went to summon the director. The old man, seated in his cubby-hole of an office in cotton trousers, string vest and grubby canvas shoes, emitted a theatrical sigh, put down his newspaper and lumbered ahead of Steve down the long corridor to the telephone.

The number which Steve had handed to the director was that of the Blue Nuns. After what appeared to be conversations with a number of different people, the old man replaced the receiver and told Steve: 'He not there.'

'Not there?' For a terrible moment Steve thought that Stefano must be dead.

'Gone. Gone home.'

'Oh!' Briefly, Steve absorbed that information. 'Then I wonder if you could now try to get me . . .?' He pulled out from the back pocket of his jeans the piece of paper, kept in a plastic folder, on which he had written down any names, addresses and telephone numbers given to him in the course of his travels.

The director closed his eyes and compressed his lips, and again emitted that theatrical sigh. He was all too clearly not pleased with his task. 'Okay. I try.' He held out his hand for the sheet of paper and Steve indicated the number. Then the director warned: 'This cost money. Operator tell how much.'

'Yes, of course.'

When the director eventually handed Steve the ancient, black bakelite receiver, it was Tilda who was on the line. 'Oh, Steve! It's you? I thought that we were never going to hear from you again.'

Her tone was cool, even tart.

'Here in Sardinia It's been difficult to get to a phone. Sorry.' But he realised the feebleness of the excuse – he was not after all in the heart of Africa – and felt a deep shame at having so patently to lie. 'How is the – er – Prince?'

The clamour from the kitchen intensified at that moment. Someone had dropped a pot, with a scream. Then everyone was shrieking with laughter. Steve strained to hear. He made out a few words: '. . . operation . . . a disaster . . . anaesthetic . . . a stroke . . .'

'So things are really bad?'

'You could say that.' Now he could hear her properly. The noise from the kitchen had subsided and so, miraculously, had the constant static on the line. 'I brought him back here from the clinic. The operation revealed what they – and I – feared. There's nothing more to be done. Things have . . . gone too far. He's too old and too ill for the horrors of chemotherapy . . . and an operation is no longer possible.'

'I'm sorry. I'm terribly sorry.'

'I tell myself that, if I had insisted on his going to Rome or Switzerland, as I begged him to do, the anaesthetic might never have caused the stroke. Who knows? Anyway, there it is. He's dying. He can't feel anything all down one side, and he has difficulty in speaking.'

'Who is looking after him?'

'Well, I am. But I also have two nurses, one for the day and one for the night, from the Blue Nuns.' The static crackled once again. Then he heard: '. . . says your name, constantly says your name.'

'He says my name?'

'Yes. All the time. Over and over. I don't know why, but he does. Says your name, over and over. I suppose it means that he . . . wants you.'

On an impulse Steve said : 'I'll come back. As soon as possible. Tomorrow. Or if not tomorrow, then just as soon –'

'Oh, you don't want to do that.'

But he did want to do it. 'I'll come. Tell him I'm coming.'

The two calls cost far more than he had thought possible. When he had queried the figure, the director glared at him indignantly and then said in his deep, croaking voice: 'Long distance. You no know? Long distance in Italy costa much, much money. Two calls,' he added.

As Steve left the little office, he decided that there was not enough time to set about trying to find a boat to carry him on that leisurely journey across the straits. He would have to fly. That would make a ruinous dent in his budget, but there was nothing else for it. He must get there as soon as possible.

In the sitting-room of the hostel, its bare, concrete floor scattered here and there with chairs and tables which looked as though they were being displayed at some provincial auction sale, Beth and Max were playing cards. Small coins stacked at their elbows, they were clearly playing for money.

Max looked up at the sound of Steve's boots scraping across the concrete. 'Where have you been? We were looking for you. We thought you might like a game of gin-rummy with us.'

'I was telephoning. My friends in Sicily.' He spoke as though they must know all about these friends, though he had never mentioned them. 'He's had a stroke. Dying. I must go back as soon as possible to see him.'

'Then the trip to Greece . . .?' Beth flashed a rueful, ironic smile. Clearly she had decided that he had thought better of travelling with them and was making an excuse. But there were no hurt feelings or rancour.

'Off, I'm afraid. I don't know when I'll be free to take up my travels again. I'm – I'm terribly sorry.' And he was terribly sorry. He always hated to let people down; and, more importantly, he had thought that Beth might eventually cure him of the constant ache of Sue's absence and indifference.

'Ah, well!' Max exclaimed. 'Ships that pass in the night.' He gathered up the scattered cards and shuffled them. 'Anyway – if you can't join us in anything else, join us in another game.'

Steve lost money to both of them. To them it seemed nothing, to him it seemed a lot.

XIV

It was Guido who eventually tugged open the cumbrous front door, in answer to the tolling of the old-fashioned bell-pull at which Steve had jerked and jerked again. Amazingly, the Italian looked far more youthful and moved far more agilely than during the whole of Steve's last visit. In the past, if one had been told that one of the household would soon die, one would have assumed it to be, not Stefano, but the ancient servant.

'*Signore! Benarrivato!*' He inclined his head and then gave a deep bow, one hand still to the door, with an irony that was far more lethal than any overt insolence. Then, as so often in the past, he stared down at Steve's soiled and scuffed boots, with a look of disdain.

Olive was with Tilda in Stefano's study. Behind the two chairs in which the two women were seated facing the door, stood Stefano's desk. Piled up on it were the innumerable pages of the novel, with the cigar-shaped, malachite pen beside them. Stefano might just have gone out for a few minutes, on one of those many visits of his to the garage between one paragraph and the next. The sight of the high stack of paper and the pen brought a pang to Steve's heart.

Tilda, who looked extraordinarily pale and haggard, struggled to her feet. Then she stepped forward, plump, white hands extended. So far from expecting a welcome of such warmth, Steve had thought, from that telephone

conversation, that she would be accusatory and bitter.
'Steve! How good of you to come! But I knew that you
would. You have a good heart. Stefano always said that.'
To his amazement, she leaned forward and kissed him on
his right cheek, at the same time clasping his hands in
hers. Her hands felt cold to the touch even on that day of
unrelenting heat.

'Well, if it isn't Steve! What a surprise!' It was Olive, not
Tilda, who, amazingly, was hostile. 'Welcome, stranger!'
Her face was mottled with red and there was the angry
beginning of a stye on her left eyelid.

Awkwardly Steve went across to her and shook her
hand.

'What can I offer you?' Tilda asked. 'A drink, some
coffee, food?'

Steve shook his head. 'I had all those things on the
plane.'

'It must have cost you a lot to fly back here.'

Embarrassed, he shook his head. 'Not all that much.'

'Of course it did! Do let me reimburse you.'

Olive's face seemed to become even more mottled, as
she squinted furiously first at Tilda and then at Steve.
What, Steve wondered, was the reason for this animosity?

'No, no!' Steve shook his head violently in rejection of
Tilda's offer.

'Stefano had another stroke last night,' Tilda said.
Suddenly her lower lip trembled and her upper lip
elongated itself, as though she were about to burst into
tears. Steve, who had always doubted whether she loved
Stefano, now knew that she did. Olive put a comforting
arm around her shoulders, drawing her to her. But, with
a jerk, Tilda pulled away. 'I hope he'll recognise you. He

seems terribly confused. And he's no longer able to say the few things that he was able to say before.'

'Like your name,' Olive put in.

'I'll see if he's sleeping. If not, I'll take you in to see him now. If that's all right for you?'

'Any time. Whenever you think best.'

Tilda disappeared with a rustling of her long skirt around her plump calves.

'The prodigal's return,' Olive said.

Steve slowly seated himself. Then, at a loss what to say in the face of this persistent hostility, he asked: 'Is the hoover working okay?'

'The *hoover?*' Olive emitted a derisive bark of laughter. 'Oh, yes, perfectly, perfectly. Maria is delighted with it.'Then she sat down in the chair opposite to his. 'He's dying, you know.'

Steve nodded. 'I imagined that.'

'Fancy delaying doing anything about all those haemorrhages merely because he wanted to finish that ridiculous book of his.'

'Perhaps it isn't ridiculous. I don't read, I don't know anything about books, but perhaps . . . It could be a best-seller.'

Olive laughed contemptuously. 'I don't think that poor old Stefano would enjoy being the author of a *best-seller.* I think that he's always played for higher stakes than that.' Then seeing the look of confusion on Steve's face, she cried out: 'You poor dear! You don't know what I'm talking about, do you?'

'I'm sorry. I don't know anything about literature.'

'Just as I don't know anything about the internal combustion engine. So that makes us quits.'

Tilda came in, followed by the largest and oldest of the Pekineses. There was a small, lace-fringed handkerchief in her right hand and with it she dabbed at her lips, as one might with a napkin after taking a sip of wine or a mouthful of food. 'He seems to be drifting in and out of consciousness. Why not come and see him? You may not get anything out of him, but still . . .'

Olive crossed over to one of the tall windows and, hand on bunched, faded green velvet curtain, frowned out into the street.

Steve mounted the stairs behind Tilda. He had never before penetrated to this storey. She opened a creaking door and he followed her into a room which contained a vast double bed with a dusty, red damask canopy sagging above it. Magazines and books were littered across it and were also piled in asymmetrical cairns on the table beside it. The atmosphere, all the windows closed, was suffocatingly close. There was exactly the same smell of disinfectant as in the youth hostel. Over a small, spindly rosewood chair, Tilda must have thrown the dressing-gown which Steve could now see. Below the chair there was a pair of mules with bedraggled pink feathers on silk of a darker pink.

Tilda turned. 'This way.' She strode across the room and opened a small door at its farther end. 'He's in his dressing-room,' she said. 'That's where he wanted to be,' she added.

Steve was amazed by the smallness and the bareness of the room, as he was by the simplicity of the narrow iron bedstead, little more than a cot, in which Stefano, eyes closed and hands resting on his chest, was lying. His face, turned up to the ceiling, appeared to be contorted by a constant grimace of anguish. A single tear glistened in the fold of a cheek. At the bottom of the bed, Mimi was sleeping. With a low growl, she raised her head and opened her eyes at the sound of their entry, then subsided back into sleep with a snuffle and grunt. Beside the bed, seated in an armchair, a nun in a heavily starched wimple, her stiff skirts reaching all but to the ground, was knitting what appeared to be the beginning of a garishly multi-coloured muffler. Behind her, Steve could just glimpse an old-fashioned wooden commode.

'Say something to him,' Tilda prompted Steve.

Steve hesitated. He had the strange sensation that everything in the little room – the medicine bottles ranged on the chimney-piece, the carafe of water and the glass on the bedside table, the ball of wool in the nun's lap – was vibrating around him. He felt his own body being shaken by the same unaccountable tremors. At last he got out, in a choked, hoarse voice: 'Stefano.' It was only the second time that he had used that name. 'Stefano!'

Stefano gave a little, bird-like cry. His eyes flickered, opened. He seemed to be gazing up at Steve in terror. The eyes rolled from side to side, as his tongue, as though it were a clapper made of lead, shifted slowly in his by now half-open mouth. 'Oh – oh – oh!' The repeated sound seemed to Steve to express the same terror as the old man's gaze.

Tilda said: 'He's trying to say your name.'

Could that really be true?

Then, with a supreme effort, the cords standing out lividly in his neck, Stefano got out a choking: 'Steve!' At the sound, the bitch again raised her head, opened her eyes, growled.

Steve leaned over him. 'Yes, Stefano. What is it? I'm here. I came back to see you. I flew from Sardinia as soon as heard you were ill.'

The eyes once more moved from side to side. Then they fixed themselves on Steve's face. Now, Steve thought, there was no terror in them, only anguish. The tongue again shifted in the half-open mouth and the Adam's apple jerked up and down. Steve took the old man's hand in his and was at once amazed by the violence of the answering grip.

'He is trying to say something to you. But . . .' The tears welled up in Tilda's eyes and, ashamed of them, she quickly turned away.

'Yes, Stefano. Yes!'

Once again, with what was clearly a superhuman effort, the old man tried to speak. The tongue lolled from side to side and a retching-like sound emerged.

'Yes!' Steve again prompted.

There is so much that I want to say to you but somehow . . .

Stefano had so often told Steve that; and now, when he was at last prepared to say it, he could not do so.

Stefano gave a little sigh. Then his eyes closed.

'I think he wants to sleep. Let's leave him now. Perhaps later . . .'

Large and serene, the nun looked up from her knitting and gave Steve a friendly smile.

'Stefano!'

There was no response.

'Later . . . You can try again later.'

But Steve somehow knew, even then, that neither he nor Stefano would ever have another opportunity to try.

*

Stefano died just as dawn was breaking the following morning.

The night-nurse, younger than the nurse whom Steve had seen, was dozing, a magazine on her knees and her mouth ajar in her square, strong, handsome, peasant face, as she rested far back, her body sideways tilted, in the huge, worn armchair.

Suddenly she had been roused by a shrill, keening sound. She had jumped to her feet, the magazine falling to the floor. Mimi was racing in demented terror round and round the room. As she did so, she spattered now the threadbare carpet and now the linoleum surrounding it with urine.

The sheet and bedclothes under Stefano's chin were soggy with blood.

His face looked peaceful but odd, one eye closed and the other open, as though he were winking. With an abrupt gesture, her breath rapidly indrawn, the nun put out a hand and sealed the open eye before she hurried out, her skirts rustling about her, to summon Tilda.

XV

In the same room which he had previously occupied,
Steve threw himself across the sagging bed. Then, face
buried in his crossed arms, he sobbed on and on, as once,
a small boy, his body similarly sprawled and his face
similarly buried, he had endlessly sobbed at some fresh
injustice or cruelty perpetrated by his father. How could
you have done that to me? he silently demanded now, as
he used silently to demand then. The only difference was
that now he demanded it in anguish, whereas at that far
distant time he had demanded it in rage. Then he had
wanted his father gone, out of the house, out of their
lives, even dead. Now he wanted Stefano back.

As he lay there, he remembered the sudden death, of
a heart-attack, of the father of that one school-fellow of
his whom he had regarded as a real friend. The boy and
he, each eight years old, had sat on the wall which
separated the small garden of the boy's home from the
road. Then, all at once, the boy had begun to cry, with
sobs which jerked agonisingly out of him, shaking his
body and twisting his mouth out of shape. Steve had
longed to console him, but he had not known how to do
so. Instead, he had watched him with what to an outsider
would have seemed to be no more than a wary,
dispassionate curiosity.

Later, back at his own home, having been cuffed
repeatedly about the head by his father, until his ears

rang, for returning so late, Steve had lain out on his bed, as he was now lying out, and had sobbed, as he was now sobbing. Then he had thought: Why couldn't his father die, suddenly, now, at this very moment, as his friend's father had died, toppling off a ladder while mending a fuse? Steve had then put forth all his will: *Die, die die!* But it was useless. Now he put forth all his will to achieve the miracle of bringing Stefano, laid out in the small, bare dressing-room, back to life: *Live, live, live!* But that too was useless.

Eventually he scrambled off the bed and made for the bathroom. He peered at himself in the blotched mirror above the wash-basin. His face looked congested, his cheeks stained with tears and his eyes red with them. His blond hair, which he had had cropped short in Sardinia for economy's sake, stuck up in tufts, which he now attempted to smooth down with a raised hand. Then he ran the cold tap. He bent over the wash-basin and splashed the icy water repeatedly over his face.

Out in the courtyard, he squatted on the rim of the fountain and, staring down at his clasped hands, listened to its intermittent lisping. He realised that his finger-nails were dirty. They had been dirty on that first evening which he had spent with Tilda and Stefano. How embarrassed he had felt when he had noticed that dirt! But now – what did it matter?

Suddenly he heard footsteps crunching on the gravel. He looked up and then waited with a queasy apprehension. Tilda, dressed in a long black dress reaching almost to the ground and with a black-and-purple silk scarf tied, even on that afternoon of intense heat, about her throat, was sailing towards him. Mimi was behind her. In her right hand Tilda was holding a khaki envelope.

Steve jumped down from his perch.

'I've brought you this.' She held out the envelope. When he did not take it, she explained: 'It's just a little money. To help you on your way – on your journey of a lifetime.'

Still he did not take it, staring at her speechless.

'Please. Please take it.'

Steve shook his head. 'It isn't necessary. Really. I have my budget.'

'But that air-ticket from Sardinia must have put your budget out completely. Please!' Then she went on: 'Stefano told me that he regretted not giving you some money when you left us. But he said – he said that he realised that what prevented him was the unconscious thought that, the less money you had, the more likelihood there was that you might eventually return.'

Steve again shook his head. There had never been any chance of his returning, except in the present circumstances.

Tilda lowered the envelope and scrutinised Steve with a fixity of gaze which made him shift his weight from one leg to the other and then look away. Once more she held the envelope out towards him. 'Please!'

At last he took it from her. 'I don't know what to say. I . . . I . . .'

'Don't say it!'

He accompanied her on her walk back over the crunching gravel to the house. By now Mimi had wandered up on to the terrace. Both of them were silent. Then, as they passed the garage, she said: 'Have you taken another look at the car?'

'No.'

'Wouldn't you like to?' She reached into the pocket of the long, black dress and took out a bunch of keys. She must have come prepared to unlock the garage door for him. She inserted the largest of the keys and turned it with difficulty, screwing up her face as she did so.

Side by side, they stared at the immensely long, highly arched, tapering bonnet.

'What is to happen to it?'

'There's this English lord. He has a motor museum. Olive met him during her last visit to England. She's written to tell him about it, with some photographs. Perhaps . . .'

It gave Steve a pang to think of the beautiful monster immobilised in a museum, like a wild animal in a cage. Perhaps the English lord would sometimes take it out of the museum and drive it?

'What time does your boat leave for Piraeus this evening?'

'Sometime late. They don't seem able to tell me exactly. Ten, eleven, twelve, they said.'

'Then you have time.' She extended the key-ring. 'Why not have a last ride?'

Steve took the key-ring from her. 'Thanks. Yes, I'd like that.'

As the car roared down the long avenue leading to the centre of the city, everyone stared at it. When it halted at some traffic-lights, a group of schoolboys, satchels in hands, raced across. One, jokingly proprietorial, posed as though for a photograph with one leg crossed over the other and his hand on the bonnet, another said something incomprehensible in Italian to the boy next to him, in a high, excited voice. Then the lights changed and the car was roaring off again.

All at once, after his afternoon of desolation over Stefano's death, Steve felt an ever-mounting exhilaration. He eased the throttle out, and then eased it out again and yet again. He was travelling at way beyond the speed limit.

He was about to pass, he realised, the main post office. Perhaps at last, at long last, there was a letter awaiting him there from Sue? In his new-found exhilaration, he was prepared to believe that. Seeing a space between a van and a Volkswagen, he deftly manoeuvred the Bugatti in. At once a crowd gathered about it, circling, pointing, smiling, commenting to each other.

It was the same clerk as on the first occasion. But this time he returned, not with that old lugubrious expression, but with a congratulatory smile. '*Ecco, signore!*'

He held out not one – that was all that Steve had dared to hope for – but a wad of envelopes. All the envelopes were of an unusual size, an extremely small rectangle, some three inches across and some two inches high, and all were made of the same thick, cream-coloured vellum. Steve went through them. Each was addressed in the same hand, a hand which he immediately recognised. '*Al egregio signore Stephen Alban*' was the superscription.

Still examining the envelopes, bewildered, uneasy, eventually fearful, Steve made his way back to the car. He clambered in. Again he went through the envelopes, even turning them over to see if there was anything written on their backs. He was reluctant to open any of them, as though to do so would be to pull the pin from a bomb.

Eventually, methodical as always, he took his Swiss army pen knife out of the pocket of his jeans and slit one of the envelopes and drew out what was in it. Then, without looking at what had been written, he slit the envelope beneath it. There were five envelopes and they contained five cards of stiff, cream-coloured board, each dated. He arranged the cards in their order of composition, realising, as he did so, that the first had been written on the day of his departure and the last on the day when Stefano had had the first of his strokes. There was a letter for each day of Steve's absence.

Even more bewildered and apprehensive, he looked at the first of the cards.

All that was written on it, under the heavily embossed family crest and the address and the date, were the three words 'I love you.' There was no signature.

Steve laid the card down on the seat beside him. He stared ahead of him through the tilted, scratched, yellowing windscreen. Everything in the street seemed to be vibrating with mounting ferocity, in time to something vibrating deep within him, in an even more disturbing repetition of his experience in the sick-room. He put a hand to his mouth and then raised it to his forehead, feeling the sweat breaking out.

Slowly, lips moving, he struggled to read the second card: 'I write a *lume spento*. Since your sun moved on, everything seems dark.' He stared at the words, uncomprehending, for a long time. *A lume spento?* What did that mean? Italian? He would never be able to ask anyone.

This card he dropped beside the other one. Again he stared ahead of him. Then he looked down at the third card. There was a hammering in his temples. It read:

> What is the opposite of love?
> Hate?
> No. Indifference.

It was a long time before Steve looked down at the fourth card. His fingers felt round its edges, then they moved over it, as though probing for something in braille. He looked down, looked away, looked down again. His mouth was half-open, the tip of his tongue caught between his teeth. Then he closed his mouth, his lips began to tremble and move:

> Wherever you are, if you are ever in any kind of difficulty, just whistle and I'll come to you.

Two workmen in paint-soiled dungarees were circling the car, pointing out now this feature and now that to each other. One of them, pot-bellied, with wiry grey hair, said something to Steve. All Steve understood was the word *bella*. He tried to smile, he nodded.

Eventually he looked at the fifth and last card:

> Bossuet wrote that to love someone too much is to do him an irreparable wrong.
> Have I done you that wrong?

Steve felt an ever-mounting horror. He had been violated by those five stiff, heavily embossed cards, each with its minuscule, copperplate writing on it; and that violation was like an echo, long delayed but now as terrifyingly reverberant as the roar of the huge monster in which he was seated, of something that had always been part of himself and of his beautiful, solitary, resistant body, even if it had never until now been a part of his conscious memory.

. . . The father has slapped the small boy back and forth across the face and then he has dragged him, screaming, off the bed and on to the floor and kicked him, kicked him repeatedly with the boots which he is wearing on his return from replacing some glass in the window of a shop which suffered a break-in the night before. As always on such occasions the boy rolls himself up into a ball, like an insect or small animal, his hands over his head. Then suddenly the father begins to weep, kneeling beside the boy. 'Sorry, boy! Sorry! Don't know what gets into me.' Tenderly he picks the boy up in his arms and lays him, paralysed now with terror out on the bed and loosens his pyjamas and then lowers his trembling hand. His lips are pressed to the side of the boy's forehead. There is a strange, terrible, bitter smell, as there is under the pepper trees on either side of the gate. The hand seems to grow and grow, it becomes a raging ravenous monster . . .

Then the unremembered became the remembered. The five stiff, heavily embossed cards had made Steve, after all those years, remember the five fingers that were the tentacles of the monster.

He scrabbled for the cards. One had fallen under his seat, another was by the gear-shift. He had to destroy them as he had to destroy the memory. Otherwise cards and memory would totally destroy him. He drove at perilous speed down the main road and then swung into a side street, where he braked to a standstill and switched off the engine. He gripped the cards in one hand and with the other tried to tear them.

But they resisted him. They seemed to have a fiendish life of their own. *Die, die., die!* But they refused to die. Eventually he took the first and tore that, then the second, then the third . . . After that, he gathered the fragments in a fist and hurled them outwards and downwards.

The wind, blowing salt, bitter and oil-laden off the sea, whirled them round and round, then lifted one, lifted another.

Steve watched the capricious dance of the fragments for a long time. Then he put his hand to the ignition key and the vast engine throbbed into life.

1997

. . . It's not right, not right at all.

Steve chews on the end of the pen and stares down at what, in his bold, childlike hand, he has written. Much of what happened he cannot remember, and even more of it he wishes that he did not remember. No, it's not right, not right at all.

To love someone too much is to do him an irreparable wrong. Did Stefano do him an irreparable wrong? Did he? Or were those days, spent with the old man and the beautiful Bugatti, the happiest of his life?

He does not want to think about it. He does not want to decide. It is all too complicated. He is contented, or almost contented, in the simplicity of a life of running this garage, of kicking a football around with the two boys and teaching the three girls to swim, of working beside Faith during the day and sleeping beside her at night. He wants nothing more. He is terrified of anything more. It is years now since he has had the Needle Dream. If he were to dream that dream again, he sometimes thinks that it would either drive him mad or make him kill himself.

He gives a grunt and pushes himself up and away from the desk.

He picks up first the letter from England and then the letter which he has so laboriously just written and begins frantically, despairingly (*Die, die, die!*) to tear up both in hands which, despite all his work in the garage, still remain as beautiful as when Stefano first saw them on a bench by a bus-stop so many years ago and so acquired the will to carry through to eventual triumph his own long, lonely, erratic journey of a lifetime.